Contents

The Year of
Abi Crim

Sharon Hambrick

JOURNEY
B O O K S ™
Greenville, South Carolina

Library of Congress Cataloging-in-Publication Data

Hambrick, Sharon, 1961-
    The year of Abi Crim / Sharon Hambrick.
        p. cm.
    Summary: Abi is certain that sixth grade will be her best year
    ever, until the favorite teacher she had hoped to have is called
    away and a new girl wins the place of concertmaster which Abi
    had thought would be hers.
    ISBN 1-57924-374-6
    [I. Schools—Fiction 2. Orchestra—Fiction 3. Violin–Fiction
    4. Christian life—Fiction.] I. Title.

PZ7.H1755 Ye 2000
[Fic]—dc21   00-020223

The Year of Abi Crim

Editor: Gloria Repp
Project Editor: Debbie L. Parker
Designed by Duane A. Nichols
Cover and illustrations by Johanna Berg

© 2000 Sharon Hambrick

ISBN 1-57924-374-6

15   14   13   12   11   10   9   8   7   6   5   4   3   2   1

in loving memory of
VERNON LUTHER
1943-1999
teacher, mentor, friend

And they that be wise
shall shine as the brightness of the firmament;
and they that turn many to righteousness
as the stars for ever and ever.
Daniel 12:3

Books by Sharon Hambrick

Arby Jenkins
Arby Jenkins, Mighty Mustang
Arby Jenkins, Ready to Roll
Stuart's Run to Faith
The Year of Abi Crim

1 Tuning Up

Abi Crim adjusted her headphones. She arranged her music on the music stand and tucked her violin under her chin. She turned the volume on the CD player up loud and placed her bow on the string, waiting for the first note. It was the last day of summer vacation, the last day before sixth grade, and her last chance to practice the Bach A Minor Concerto with the great violinist Jascha Heifetz before orchestra auditions tomorrow.

She knew it was ridiculous of her to have thought she could learn this piece of music. It was far too difficult for an eleven-year-old kid, even one who had been playing the violin since she was seven years old. But begin the piece she had, back in June, the day fifth grade ended.

All summer she had practiced this concerto, playing along with the CD, over and over until she heard it in her mind all day long. No, she wasn't as good as Heifetz, never would be, but then again, how many people were? Besides, Heifetz was dead, along with most of the great violinists whose faces looked out at her from the poster on her bedroom wall.

Nicolo Paganini? Dead long ago. The greatest violinist of all time, some people said. They said he could play full concerts on just one string. Yehudi Menuhin, also dead. Fritz

Kreisler, dead. But some were still living. Isaac Stern, Pinchas Zukerman, Itzhak Perlman.

And me, Abi Crim.

Abi began to play, the music pouring into her ears. She cringed at the sound coming from her instrument and stopped playing. She punched the off button and hung her headphones on the music stand next to the sheet music. She looked over at her poster.

I bet none of them had trouble learning to tune up.

Tuning took so much time. You had to walk out to the living room, play the A above middle C on the piano and then, while the note lingered on the air, you twisted the A string's tuning peg up a little or down a little so that when the bow was drawn across the A string, it matched the A on the piano.

It was no problem, really, but Abi disliked the trouble it was to turn off the CD player, remove the headphones, take the instrument out to the living room, and so on.

"Why don't you tune up first, before you begin?" Mom had asked not so long ago.

Abi shrugged her shoulders. "I just figure the strings will be in tune, I guess."

Mom said "Ah," and gave her a look that was full of meaning.

Now, Abi tuned her violin carefully, first her A string, then the other strings, playing the A with the D and listening carefully for the interval, like a real musician. Like Heifetz. Adjust the D until it sounds exactly right. Then play the D and G together and adjust the G. Finally, she played the A string and the E string, the highest string, together. Perfect.

Back in her room, she turned Heifetz up loud and played along through the whole first movement of the concerto. Her mind filled with visions of the audience she imagined before her, the audience that hung on her every note and who sat astonished at her sheer ability, entranced by the perfection of her sound. Imagined applause filled her ears as she pulled the final note of the movement, a clear, perfect A. She smiled and bowed slightly.

"Abi?"

"What?" Abi turned quickly to her bedroom door. "Oh, Kimberly, it's you. Come in."

Kimberly Edison lived across the street from Abi, and the two girls were best friends. They played music together—Kimberly on the piano, Abi on the violin. They went to church together. They went on each other's family vacations together. Everything they did, they did together, except for one thing: school.

"Ready for school tomorrow?" Kimberly said.

"Yep." Abi smiled. "It's my year, Kimberly. It is the year of Abi Crim." She laid her violin gently in the velvet-lined case and grinned. "I'm going to get straight As again. And I am almost positive I'm going to be concertmaster."

"First violin?"

"Yep," she twirled around. "Very first violin, top of the orchestra, best of the best." She flopped down onto her bed. "I'm going to be Mr. Doyle's right-hand girl. I can't wait to stand up in front of the orchestra at the Christmas concert and play my A string so everyone else can tune their instruments to it. You're coming to the concert, aren't you?"

"Of course. I always come to your concerts. Concerts and museums are what we do. You know that."

Both girls laughed, but Abi wasn't sure whether she envied Kimberly or felt sorry for her. Kimberly hadn't gone to school in two years. Instead, she'd studied with her mother at home.

"Do you like home schooling?" Abi asked for the hundredth time.

"Mostly," Kimberly said. "But it can be lonely sometimes."

"School can be lonely sometimes too," Abi said.

"Yeah, but Stephen Carpenter's there," Kimberly said. She jabbed Abi in the ribs with her elbow and laughed.

"Hey, no fair," Abi said. "There aren't any boys at your school for me to tease you about."

Mom poked her head into the room. "Abi, I need you to make the meatloaf for me, okay, Sweetie?"

Abi sighed. "Okay, Mom." She turned to Kimberly. "Meatloaf is my specialty. Want to stay and watch?"

"No, thanks. Raw meat gives me the creeps."

"See you after school tomorrow then," Abi said. "By then I'll be concertmaster."

Abi's brother Will, sixteen, talkative, and thinking about the Air Force, was stabbing potatoes with a fork when Abi ran into the kitchen.

"You're doing potatoes?"

"Myself," he said. "But don't worry. There's no rush for us to get dinner ready. Dad had an emergency school board meeting, so he'll be late getting home. That means I have time to learn how to stab potatoes and put them on the oven rack."

He laughed and rubbed Abi's head, messing up her hair.

"Don't do that, or I'll throw globs of raw hamburger on you."

Will moved farther from her. "Okay, I know. To pass the time, let's play, 'Why are they having a school board meeting the day before school starts?'"

"Maybe the school is on fire," Abi said.

Will laughed. "That's a good one. Here's one: maybe all the teachers quit." He opened the oven door and placed the potatoes on the rack. "That would be great, if the teachers quit. No more school!"

"Not good," Abi said. "No school means no orchestra."

Will washed his hands and wiped them on the towel. "Speaking of orchestra, that reminds me. To make up for all the times I didn't practice all summer, I figure I have to practice one-hundred twenty-five hours tonight."

"You can't practice that much in one night," Abi said. "There aren't enough hours. Besides, no one plays the cello better than you."

"You never know," Will said, turning to leave the kitchen. "New kids come every year."

Abi gathered the ingredients for meatloaf around her like familiar friends. She loved the way the meat and oatmeal and eggs and onion-soup mix squeezed through her fingers in oozy globs, so cold it hurt her hands. Then, when the meat was mashed into the loaf pan and slid into the oven, she always washed her hands for a long time in hot soapy water.

She set the oven timer for fifty-five minutes, then sat down at the computer. As she clicked on the e-mail program and began to write, she heard Will's cello scales two rooms away.

Dear Grandma, (she wrote)

Tomorrow school starts! I'll get Mr. Doyle at last. He's the best teacher at Fairlawn Christian School, and I get him at last! He teaches sixth grade. He also teaches orchestra after school. I have a secret about orchestra. I'll tell you later. Dad had an emergency school board meeting. Maybe the school burned down. Ha ha. If it did, maybe I can home school like my friend Kimberly. How's Ludwig?

Dad's car drove up, so Abi wrote *Love, Abi* quickly and punched the send button. Grandma would write back. She always did.

"Hi, Punkin."

"Hi, Dad." She jumped up for her nightly bear hug and got her hair messed up by Dad's big hand.

She was certain her father was the best dad in the world. He was tall and broad like a well-built ship, sturdy and seaworthy. He played Frisbee with her in the back yard and helped her practice recital pieces by listening with full attention, not listening while also reading *The Wall Street Journal.*

He looked a little strange in the face tonight, as if maybe the school had burned down and the school board was trying desperately to figure out what to do with hundreds of kids the next morning. After he'd talked to Mom for a few minutes in their room, Mom looked strange too, like she had heard terrible news.

Probably nothing. Everything's going to be fine. It's going to be my year. The year of me.

Not that her parents would tell her the school board news. They hardly ever did.

"You can learn all the news when everyone else does," Dad had said once, grinning widely. "I don't want anyone to think I'm bringing school problems home for you to solve, Miss Abigail Crim."

Abi laughed at that. As if Dad ever had a problem he couldn't solve all by himself. He could figure anything out. How to fix the car, for example. Or the stove or the plumbing. Dad could do anything. He even saved lives every day at work.

Mom lit the dinner table candles just like every other night—"any night with my family is worth lighting candles," Mom said—and Abi bowed her head. Dad thanked God for the day, the food, the family, and mostly, Dad said, for the great Redeemer, the Lord Jesus Christ.

Outside, the daylight had begun to fade, but inside, the candles flicked bright fire as Dad talked of church and politics and work at the hospital: two babies had come in today, both tiny, both sick. Then he looked at Abi.

"School tomorrow, Punkin." His voice seemed strained, but Abi wasn't worried. She smiled at him. "Yep," she said.

Abi let the talk waft around her as she buttered another roll. In her mind she held up and examined each piece of the Mr. Doyle legend.

He drove a 1957 teal blue Chevrolet convertible. He wore suspenders, bow ties, and derby hats. He brought glazed donuts for his class sometimes, and when he turned forty, he had thrown a pizza party for the whole elementary school. Abi had only been in second grade then, but she still remembered the pepperonis and the smile on his face when the whole school sang "Happy Birthday to You."

She had longed most to be in his class back in the fourth grade when her teacher made the students do toe touches and jumping jacks by their desks when they weren't paying proper attention to the lessons. It seemed that this mostly happened on bright days when the outside called through the shut-tight windows, begging the children to come and play, while the teacher was chalking down methods for determining whether to say *sit* or *set, lie* or *lay*.

"Abigail," Mom said, "Dad asked you a question."

"Sir?" Abi said, turning to Dad.

"I asked if you were excited about seeing your friends again tomorrow?"

"Yes," Abi said, "And Mr. Doyle."

"Ah," said Dad, "Mr. Doyle."

"And also," she said, her voice tensing with excitement, "I think I can be concertmaster." A large smile spread over her face. "My vibrato is good. My tuning is good. I can even play the A Minor Concerto."

Her family applauded. Abi clamped her smile into a tight grin, but her eyes were bright.

"I can never be concertmaster," Will said. "Me and my poor little cello. Doomed to the other side of the stage. I think I'll join the Air Force and fly planes instead."

Abi laughed. Will was her favorite person in the world. He made silly comments to her all the time, but at least he didn't put worms in her pillowcase anymore. And then there was his music. He played the cello with deep, fervent tones, rich vibrato, and long bows, tip-to-frog, that she loved to watch, measure after measure. It was his love of music—listening to him play his cello hour after hour when she was little—that cemented the dream of music in her heart. Listening to Will and remembering Grandpa.

Grandpa. Her first and favorite musician. He played the bassoon. When Abi was little, she refused to go to sleep until the tape recording of Grandpa playing lullabies on the great wind instrument had played from beginning to end, enveloping her in Grandpa's music. She still had the tape, but didn't play it often. It was underneath her bed in the box that said *My Special Treasures* in gold crayon.

She sighed. She might never be as good a musician as either Will or Grandpa. But she could be concertmaster.

"Would you be called *concertmaster* or *concert-mistress?*" Mom's voice broke in.

"Concertmaster," Abi said. "Mr. Doyle says *concert-master* doesn't need to be adjusted for gender."

"Well, then, if Mr. Doyle said it, we'll see," said Dad.

"Don't worry, Abi; you'll be great no matter what they call you." said Will. He took a second potato and slathered butter on it that melted into yellow rivers. "Once there was a woman who was king of Egypt. She even wore a beard."

2 Disappointment

The next morning while Abi was getting dressed, she heard the phone ring. Dad's deep voice answered, but she couldn't understand the words through the wall. She made a face at her reflection in the mirror and wondered if she would always be so skinny, and if her thin blonde hair would ever be long and full like Mom's. She pulled her hair back into a ponytail and tied it with a red ribbon, but then wondered whether, now that she was a sixth grader, she was too old for red ribbons.

"You look good," Mom said. Abi and Will waited by the door, ready to go.

"We look the same as always," Will said.

"You look great," Mom said, patting Will on the arm. "So grown-up and wonderful."

Mom kissed Abi good-bye.

"Abi," Mom said, "I'll be praying for you today. Do your best whatever happens."

"I will, Mom," Abi said.

Out on the sidewalk, she skipped ahead.

"Hold on a minute, Sis," Will said. "Remember I'm lugging a cello here!"

She looked at Will and smiled. She was only moments away from the best year of her life, everything falling into its proper place at last: good friends, a great teacher, and hope-fully—probably—the concertmaster's chair. She would do her best in her schoolwork to please Mom and Dad and Mr. Doyle. She would practice hard and behave herself. She would be a good example to her friends and the younger kids. She would be concertmaster. She would—

"Did you hear me, Sis?" Will's voice broke in on her thoughts.

"No," Abi said, "sorry."

"I said, 'Are you scared? Is the big bad day closing in on my little sister?'"

Abi laughed. "Nope," she said. "Why should I be scared? I'm happy. I get Mr. Doyle at last."

She was almost in his class. Just down the street and around the corner and then she'd be there. She remembered Will telling her that Mr. Doyle passed out chocolate kisses whenever the class did especially well on something—like when everyone got the memory verse right or the time one of his students won Best of Show at the science fair. Abi de-cided to work hard so that Mr. Doyle would give her class candy for something she'd done.

"Oops. Me and my fat mouth," Will said. "I overheard Mom and Dad talking this morning, but I guess it's supposed to be a secret." His voice sounded strangely faint.

"What's a secret?" Abi asked. Had Mr. Doyle been told he couldn't give candy anymore? Had someone complained to the school board that candy was not good for children? Had that been the reason for the emergency school board meeting yesterday?

Will stopped walking and stared down at Abi from his five-foot-nine inches of big-brotherness. He put his hand on her shoulder, steadying her, as if she were a fragile piece of china ready to be dropped and shattered.

"Mr. Doyle had to fly to Minnesota yesterday, Sis. His father is very ill and has no one else to care for him. Mr. Doyle may be gone a long time."

"But . . ." Abi couldn't frame the sentence she wished to speak.

"Who . . ." Tears she didn't want and couldn't wish away filled up her eyes and dropped over onto her hot face.

"I don't know." Will touched her arm. "Sorry," he said.

They walked on in silence. Abi's backpack hung heavy on her shoulder, and she clutched tightly at the handle of her violin case.

3 Mrs. Cotton

A nervous hush followed the hubbub of hellos and hugs as the sixth-grade students found their places. Their names stared back at them in Mr. Doyle's inch-high printing from name tags taped to the tops of the desks. Abi slid into her chair and nestled her violin case under her desk. She waited, jittery.

A new girl sat in front of Abi. Her name tag said *Tamika Mitchell*. She was a tall, slender girl with skin the color of Mom's coffee—two creams and a sugar. Abi counted seventeen braids in Tamika's pitch-black hair, dotted with green and blue plastic beads. Tamika had a violin case under her desk, too, and for a moment, a tiny fear pattered into Abi's heart.

No problem. She can't be as good as me.

There were fourteen boys and eleven girls waiting and wondering. The clock ticked each second. The bell rang. Eight o'clock. No teacher.

Stephen Carpenter walked to the front of the room. It was like him to do this, and it both embarrassed and pleased Abi to see him take control of the situation.

"I'm going to get things started," he said. "Somebody's got to, and we don't seem to have a teacher."

Abi fidgeted in her seat, wondering whether she should say something about Mr. Doyle's trip to Minnesota. She looked around the room and noticed that none of the other girls wore ribbons in their hair. She undid her ponytail and fluffed her hair out.

"Do it, Steve-man," Jerry's voice boomed. "The pledge, the pledge."

"I know what to do, Jerry," Stephen said. "Everybody stand up."

The class stood and pledged their allegiance to the American flag. Then to the Christian flag and to the Bible.

"I will now take roll," Stephen said. "When I point to you, tell me your name, and I will write it down."

Stephen pointed to the first desk in the first row.

"You know me, Steve."

"State your name, please," Stephen said. Stephen wanted to be a lawyer when he got older, and it had often seemed to Abi that he was embarrassed not to be older now.

"Martin Eberhard."

"Fine. Next."

"Jerry Walters the Second."

"Candy Wong."

"Filbert Cheesehead." Everyone laughed at Zack for saying this, but Stephen fixed him with a fierce look.

"Is that Filbert with a *Ph* or an *F?*" Stephen said.

"Hey," Zack said, "don't write that down. I'm me, Zack Parker, like always."

Stephen wrote for a few seconds, then looked up and pointed at the next seat.

"Li-Chiu Harris."

"Tamika Mitchell."

Abi's face felt hot when Stephen pointed to her.

"Your name, please." She felt as if Stephen was a prosecuting attorney, not a boy she had known since she was four years old.

"Abi Crim."

"Full name, please."

"Abigail Jane Crim, your honor."

Stephen looked up, smiled faintly, then stopped.

The door had opened. Abi's head snapped left. She heard Stephen plop down in his seat two rows off. Time stopped.

A tall, dark woman—the color of Grandma Johnson's best brownies—stood in the doorway for an instant, then silently moved to the lectern. Her walk was graceful, fluid, as if she were not walking at all, but gliding across the floor.

The woman glanced over Stephen's roll-list and then, looking from face to face, she found Abi's face, locked eyes as if she knew her—that her name was the last name on the list—and nodded to the girl behind her, not speaking.

"Jillian Red Crow."

"Kristy Seward."

"Thomas Pike."

"Mindy Rossman," and so on, until the class list was complete.

"Please forgive me for arriving late," the lady said. "It won't happen again."

She looked around the room in a gaze that encompassed them all.

"My name," she said, "is Mrs. Cotton. Mrs. Iris Cotton. I am twenty-nine years old. Mr. Cotton and I have been married for seven years, and although we have no children, we do have a dog named Wilberforce."

Mrs. Cotton tilted her head to one side as if she were thinking.

"Well," she said, "as those are the answers to the usual questions, I do not expect, nor will I answer any further questions concerning my personal life. Is this clear?"

Twenty-five heads moved up and down. Perfectly clear.

"I always require a spoken answer of my students, please," she said.

Twenty-seven replies: "Yes, ma'am."

Mrs. Cotton's smile was wide. Her dress was orange and yellow and green, a riot of color. She wore red lipstick and wide gold-hoop earrings. Like sunshine, she moved up and down the classroom aisles as she spoke, her voice smooth, yet clear and confident.

Abi gazed at her in wonder.

"Naturally," she said, handing out math books and directing the class to turn to page one, "I was surprised to get such an interesting job offer in the middle of the night. It isn't often the telephone rings with someone offering exactly the position you'd most desire: teach sixth grade and conduct a string orchestra after school. No," she flashed a smile of brilliant cheerfulness. "It was a thing to pray over. Mr. Cotton and I talked and prayed. And here I am."

During recess, the sixth-grade girls gathered in small clumps, slow-munching their snacks, speaking in whispers, though the field was wide and they could not be overheard.

"She's beautiful," Abi said.

"She's wonderful," Kristy said.

"She's black," said Jerry, sidling up to a group of girls. "Or didn't you notice?"

"We noticed," Abi said, "having eyes."

"Well, then," he said, "I guess the school was pretty desperate."

"Don't be an idiot, Jerry," Candy said. "This is the twenty-first century, unlike the one you live in," but Jerry laughed like a man who had won a prize. Abi stared after him as he ran away. Her mouth hung open. What if Mrs. Cotton heard him say something like that? She wondered if Mrs. Cotton would cry.

"Ignore him," Katie said. "He's a slug."

Abi wished that, like a slug, Jerry would disappear under a rock somewhere.

After recess, Mrs. Cotton led the class in the usual first-day-of-school things, like everyone introducing themselves and telling how many people lived in their homes, how many years they had attended Fairlawn Christian, and what they had done during the summer months.

"I went to the ocean with my friend Kimberly," Abi said.

"I went to the mall a lot," Mindy said.

"I got a new violin. And I went to music camp," said Tamika. "I got to stay four weeks. It was wonderful."

A surge of worry swelled in Abi's heart. This Tamika person might be very very good after all. *Good enough to beat me?*

Time passed quickly as Mrs. Cotton passed out textbooks, rearranged seating, discussed classroom rules. At two-fifty-five, she smiled.

"Well, we've done it," she said. "Our first day." She smiled at the whole class, and Abi felt warmed-up and happy.

"Please write down your homework assignment," Mrs. Cotton said. "You are to write a nice paragraph using ten of your spelling words. That'll be enough work for the first night."

Mrs. Cotton closed the day by praying for safety, good rest, and that they all would grow to love Jesus more.

"Now have a nice afternoon," she said. "You orchestra people go to the auditorium. Be tuned up and ready to play when I get there."

When Abi reached the door, backpack over her shoulder, violin case in hand, Mrs. Cotton patted her on the back. "I'll see you in a few minutes, Abigail."

The music room was loud with the thud of backpacks hitting the floor, the clunk of instrument cases opening, the scrape of chairs on the floor. Then the first strains of music sounded as major scales filled the room. Abi smiled and played a two-octave D-major scale, pulling full bows, sliding up to third position on her E string for the last four notes, shaking vibrato from her hand like waves of gladness.

She stood alone, knowing her warm-up was being watched by curious fourth graders on their first-ever day of orchestra.

She loved to stand apart like this, pretending she was playing to thousands, drowning in thunderous applause. She played through a few pieces she had memorized. Then Abi noticed, out of the corner of her eye, Tamika at the piano, tuning. She thunked a note on the piano, plucked her string and listened, and then twisted the peg, tuning. Tamika did this with all four strings, and Abi grinned. Abi could tune like a real musician—like Jascha Heifetz—playing two strings at once, listening for the interval. As if to prove this to the room—in her mind the assembled musicians had become a starstruck audience—she played her A string, then her A and D together, listening, adjusting her D down half a step. Then the D and G, adjusting the G down a notch. Finally, her A and E together, loosening the fine tuner on her E string just a bit.

Then, just as Mrs. Cotton called for the students' attention, Abi slid into the seat next to Tamika.

"All tuned?" Mrs. Cotton asked.

Abi smiled as she replied along with everyone else, "Yes, ma'am."

Tamika plucked her strings softly, soundlessly, as Mrs. Cotton introduced herself to the fourth and fifth graders. She explained that Mr. Doyle would have loved to have been there, but his father was gravely ill. Perhaps he'd be back sometime this semester, perhaps not.

Tamika wiped her hands alternately on her skirt, leaving little smudges of sweat, and Abi felt happy at her apparent nervousness. Maybe Tamika was good, even very good, but the fact was she had not tuned like a real violinist tuned, and what good were four weeks of music camp if one hadn't even learned to tune up!

If she's very good, she can sit second chair, next to me.

"You'll be fine," she whispered. Tamika nodded.

"Instruments up." Mrs. Cotton's voice cut through her thoughts. Abi tucked her violin under her chin.

"Major scale. Begin on open G. One, two, three, and . . ."

The slow scale filled the room—G, A, high B finger, C touching B, open D, E, F-sharp touching G and back down again.

Abi cringed. Much of the orchestra seemed to be untuned. Even Tamika, for all her meticulous tuning, was sharp. Abi could hear the difference between them distinctly. Tamika did, however, have a rich, wide vibrato.

After the scales, Mrs. Cotton called the fourth-grade violinists to the front of the room. The seven of them stood in a straight, trembling line, sawing jerky strokes on half-sized instruments. A loud squawk split the air. Many giggles. One beet-red face. And Mrs. Cotton saying, Never mind, things happen.

The fifth graders were next. Major scales, then minor scales, an arpeggio—slow, then fast, then really fast until they laughed. Mrs. Cotton asked two of them to sight-read a piece she'd brought. An easy Mozart arrangement, Abi thought.

Finally, the sixth graders were called. Abi looked out at the crowd—no longer a crowd, really, since many of the younger kids had left after their auditions—and pictured a far bigger one, the one that would hear them at the Christmas Concert. Thinking this, she did not hear Mrs. Cotton's instructions.

"What did she say?" she whispered to Mindy who stood next to her.

"C major, two octaves."

"No talking on stage, please."

Abi blushed.

Pay attention. This thing's not decided yet.

They played the scale. Up and down. Slow and fast. She thought the scale sounded strange. Funny, like everyone was out of tune except her.

Then Mrs. Cotton called each of the sixth-grade violinists in turn.

"Please understand this will take a bit of time," she said to the violas, cellos, and basses. "I have to hear each sixth-grade violinist to determine specific seats."

Mrs. Cotton placed a chair for herself about a yard from the music stand where she could see the music. She sat with her pen poised over her clipboard.

"The music you will play for me now is the solo section that the concertmaster will play at the Christmas concert this year. Mr. Doyle chose this music, and I'm happy to say it's one of my favorite Christmas pieces, "Thou Didst Leave Thy Throne." I'd like you to think of the words while you play:

Thou didst leave Thy throne and Thy kingly crown,
When Thou camest to earth for me;
But in Bethlehem's home was there found no room
For Thy holy nativity.
O come to my heart, Lord Jesus,
There is room in my heart for Thee.

"Think of the sacrificial love the Savior had for us to leave heaven on our pitiful accounts. Play with that feeling in mind."

Mindy played first. She was good. Thomas next, then Candy. Abi hoped she would be last so she could leave the audience with a true sense of how the hymn could be played, full bowings and deep meaning.

"Abigail."

At last, the moment had come that she had dreamed of for years: the moment when she would play for first chair—concertmaster. She looked at the piece: common time, a simple melody of quarter notes and eighth notes. Nothing fancy. It would be enough to play it with deep, rich feeling.

She nodded to Mrs. Fowler, the pianist, and began.

Something was wrong. Abi's heart beat hard—she seemed to be flat on every note. A full half-step flat. She had to adjust her fingering on every note. The quick slides up were noticeable, she was sure, and she tried to make up for it by a good vibrato and full bows. It was no use. The piano was sharp, she determined. Then—like a lightning flash—her stupidity, overwhelming stupidity flowed over her in floods of shame. Hot tears fell while she finished the piece.

She hadn't tuned to the piano. She had tuned to her own A string.

Tamika's brilliant playing surrounded her as her heart ached. She didn't stay to hear the cellos and basses audition.

4 Consolation

There was no one who could console Abi like Kimberly could, and Abi got to Kimberly's house as fast as she could that afternoon. She plopped herself down on the front porch swing and told the whole terrible story, her violin case across her lap like a naughty child waiting to be spanked.

"It was my own fault," Abi said. "I was stupid."

"I've been stupid."

"True."

"Hey, wait a minute. When was I stupid?"

"Many times, but never as stupid as me today. Can you believe I didn't check the A on the piano before tuning? I was totally off key. I don't think I can go back to school ever again. I'm going to join your home school."

Abi hung her head over her instrument. She scuffed the ground with her feet as it passed under them—*scoosh, scoosh*—while they swung. She was glad for a friend like Kimberly—always there, always on her side.

"Everything will be okay," Kimberly said. "In a few weeks, you won't even remember this."

"I'll remember it until I'm a hundred and ten."

"You'll be dead by then, so it won't be a problem."

"Hey!"

"Don't worry about it," Kimberly said, flipping her long black hair over her shoulder in a way Abi envied.

"Probably Mrs. Cotton will take it all into consideration and give you the second chair."

"Do you think so?"

"Probably."

"Then again," she said, "it wasn't only Tamika who was better than me. It was everyone."

"This could be a problem," said Kimberly. "But never mind." She picked up a small stone from the brick step and tossed it arcing into the back yard. It landed in the bird-bath—*plonk*—and sank.

"How can I never mind?" Could she never mind that her hope of concertmaster was dashed? Never mind that she had imagined herself tossing off a stellar performance and had ended up hurling off-key notes instead?

"Hmm," said Kimberly. She sat on the step silently, gazing out across the back yard and into the field beyond. "Let's predict."

"Okay," Abi said, mechanically, knowing her friend had suggested their favorite game in order to take her mind off the bad situation.

"I predict that in eight or nine years you'll play in the first violin section in the University symphony," said Kimberly, speaking softly, surely.

"Really?"

"Really."

"Not concertmaster?"

"Maybe concertmaster," she said, "but probably not. People come from all over the world to the University."

"Maybe concertmaster, though?"

"Maybe."

"First violins for sure?"

"For sure. You're really good."

They stared across the carefully kept front lawn.

"Thank you, Kimberly."

"And me," she said. "I will sip iced tea."

"Amid the coconut palms," Abi said.

"Under the tropical sun," she said.

"Of Waikiki," they said together.

"And I shall walk along Kalakaua Avenue in a sky blue muumuu, humming to myself of far-off Tahitian shores."

Abi looked at her in surprise. "Why wish for Tahiti if you're already in Honolulu?"

Kimberly shot Abi a wicked glance. "Why wish for concertmaster if you're already in the symphony?"

"I—uh, well, because," Abi said, fumbling, "because concertmaster is the best. It's my dream."

"One can always dream," Kimberly said, getting up, smoothing her dark-blue denim skirt and laughing.

Abi picked up her backpack and violin to go home. Kimberly pulled at her sleeve. "Hey," she said, "it's okay. Your audition, I mean. It'll be okay."

"I know," Abi said. "It'll be okay nine years from now. But right now it's very much horrible and not okay."

She walked through Kimberly's den with its hunter green walls and the vase that came from Hong Kong, through the hall lined with pictures of Kimberly at every stage of her life. She stopped for a second before the mirror in the entryway, disliking the day-weary reflection of herself, then hunched her backpack to a more comfortable position and walked out into the afternoon.

It was five o'clock by the time she got home. Just in time to set the table.

"Use the china," Mom said. Abi wondered why. Mom's china was for special occasions, like Christmas. Or special events, like when Dad got his master's degree or when Mom lost twenty-five pounds in time for her high school reunion. Maybe Mom wanted the china out to celebrate her audition.

"No china, Mom. I did a terrible job," she said. "I was awful."

Mom came over and hugged her close, smoothing her hair and kissing the top of her head.

"I know," she said. "I heard."

"Then why the china?" Abi said, wondering how Mom always knew everything.

"The china is for you, Abi," Mom said. "We love you no matter how your auditions go."

Abi smiled halfheartedly. Then she peeked in at the fish, steaming in the hot spice that made her mouth hurt when she took a too-big bite. She washed her hands and set the table, two forks each when Mom used the china.

Dad looked tired when he came to the dinner table. He stirred his coffee, peppered his salad, and gazed at Mom across the bouncing candle flame.

Will plopped down in his seat and placed a can of soda pop at his place. "Teenagers need soda," he said. "It's essential to our lives and social development."

No one replied. Will said, "Okay, let's get this show on the road," and then Mom announced that it was Abi's turn to ask God's blessing on the meal.

"Dear God, Thank you for the food." A long pause, then, "Amen."

Everyone looked at her, so she looked down and began to stir her food around on her plate.

"Something wrong, Sis?" Will said. "You look awful. Is it your new teacher? Does she have fangs?"

"Oh, yes," Dad said. "How is Mrs. Cotton?" It seemed to Abi that his voice was disconnected from his thoughts, like he was forcing himself back to the dinner table and into the family.

"She's fine. But my orchestra audition was horrible."

"What happened?" Will asked. "Are you saying that my little sister did not make concertmaster?"

"No," she said. For a moment she sat in silent grief. Then, with shaking sobs, she managed, little by little, to tell the story.

"I was so proud and sure of myself," she said. "I thought I'd show those little fourth graders how a real violinist tunes. You know, two strings at a time. But I didn't take the time to walk over to the piano. It was on the other side of the room, anyway. I figured my A would be in tune. So, I tuned to my own A string."

It took her a long time to say this, and the explanation was punctuated with little gasps and hard swallowings.

"And since your A string was off, all your strings got off," said Will. He sighed deeply. "That is a seriously bad situation. I am deeply grieved for you in this predicament. It will probably hang like lead around your neck for the next seventy-five years."

"Will," Mom said, "that's enough."

Abi wiped her eyes with her fist. She blew her nose on a napkin.

The phone rang, and Dad jumped like he'd been shot. "I'll get it," he said. "It's the unit."

Dad was a nurse practitioner in the neonatal intensive care unit at Fairlawn General Hospital. That meant he worked with very small, very sick babies. Some of Abi's friends thought it was strange that her dad was a nurse, but to her it was normal. Dad had always been a nurse.

Abi loved to go to the unit—NICU, they called it—to see the tiny preemies hold on to life. She and Mom went to the NICU sometimes to take Dad lunch. She had to walk quietly and not say anything, but once she had seen a one-pound baby and had gasped out loud at its tinyness. Dad often brought home happy stories from NICU: a baby was much better, or had learned to drink from a bottle—instead of having a tube run down its nose into its stomach—or had smiled. Or got to go home at last. But then, sometimes, a baby would not get better.

Dad's voice on the phone was muffled, coming from the next room. Abi could hear only short one-syllable sounds like "Oh" and "hmm."

"Maybe the new teacher—what's her name, Mrs. Linen?—will still put you in the first violin section," Will said. "That would be all right, wouldn't it?"

"Maybe. I guess so," she said. "But even some of the fifth graders were better than me. At least they played in tune!"

"But your technique is so much better than theirs," he said. "Mrs. Polyester will see that."

Dad slumped back into his seat at the dinner table. His eyes glistened wet.

"What is it, Mark?" Mom said. "Is it bad news?"

"That was the hospital," he said. "Baby Betsy died."

"Oh no," said Mom, putting her fork down. "What happened?"

"She crashed."

Crashed, Abi had learned, meant that a baby's vital signs—blood pressure, breathing, pulse rate—got real bad really fast.

"Dr. Miller worked on her for half an hour, but there wasn't anything he could do. X-rays showed a collapsed lung, along with other things."

Dad stirred his food around on his plate with his fork.

"I'm so sorry," Mom said.

Dad got up, his food uneaten. He looked at Mom apologetically.

"Sorry about not eating," he said. "I'm going back to the hospital. I might be able to help."

"I know," said Mom.

Dad walked around the table and hugged Mom goodbye. Then he patted Abi's head and leaned down.

"You're the best violinist I know," he whispered in her ear.

They had devotions without Dad. Abi knew he'd driven to the hospital in case he'd get a chance to pray with Baby Betsy's parents, to share again with them the news of the Redeemer. *The Redeemer* was Dad's favorite name for Jesus.

"Redemption is what He's done for me," Dad would say.

Mom read First Peter chapter two. Abi felt small and silly, her audition-catastrophe fading into nothingness in comparison to Dad's real-life sorrow. She would still be in orchestra tomorrow. Baby Betsy would not be back to give her parents a hope for one more breath, one more heartbeat.

Having your conversation honest among the Gentiles: that, whereas they speak against you as evildoers, they may by your good works, which they shall behold, glorify God in the day of visitation.

Mom stopped at this verse and read it twice.

"Will," she said, "please talk about this verse."

Even though Will was often silly, he was serious during family devotions. "It means we should always be honest and good so God will be glorified."

"Right," she said. "Abi, does it say we must always be the best or greatest at our personal hobby?" She said it quietly, but it pierced Abi's heart.

Abi hung her head. "No, Mom. But I wanted to win so much."

"I know."

Mom cuddled up with Abi later in her bed. She did this often. In the dark it was easy to talk about things like how old did you have to be to date, and what do you do when you're home alone and the telephone rings, and what will heaven be like, and how long is forever.

"Were you ever humiliated, Mom?"

"Oh, Abi, you have not begun to be humiliated. This thing today, it was nothing, just a mistake. Now me? I know embarrassment. Trust me."

Her voice sounded embarrassed, and though Abi couldn't see Mom's face in the darkness next to her, she could feel in her bones that Mom was turning red with hot shame.

"What, what?"

"I can't tell you," Mom said. Then, "Aauggh!"

"What? Tell me!"

"Okay," she said. But didn't tell.

"Okay," she said again. "I will tell you about a few times. For example, once I wore a shirt inside out for a whole day of teaching!"

"All day?"

"All day. All through class. All through teachers' meeting. All through afternoon violin lessons. Nobody told me."

"That's terrible."

"Another time I wore two different earrings."

"That's bad."

"Another time, there was a chocolate cake in the church kitchen. Some of us teachers were in there during recess and decided it was for us. While we were eating it, an old woman hobbled in and said, 'Why are you eating my funeral cake?' "

Abi laughed. "That's awful."

"It's not the worst thing."

"What? What?"

"Once," Mom said, her voice full of stern foreboding, "I wore two curlers in my hair to church. I had been in a great hurry that morning, and, well, I wasn't careful. One can only see the front of one's head, after all."

Mom kissed Abi and strode out of the room.

The next morning Abi congratulated Tamika. The words, *Congratulations, Tamika Mitchell, concertmistress!* were written in green and blue marker on the front white board.

"Thank you," she said. "And I'm sorry too."

"It's okay," Abi said. "It was my own fault, and I learned a lesson."

Mom had told her the lesson at breakfast that morning.

Abi had been eating cereal with one hand and writing her spelling homework with the other. She had forgotten the homework until then. Fortunately, though, settling spelling words into paragraphs was a long-standing tradition at Fairlawn Christian School, and she knew the routine.

First, she listed her chosen words at the top of the page: *adversary, truncate, enthusiastic, botany, vilify, alternate, various, mountainous, ethereal, vague.*

"Honey," Mom said, "have you thought about what God might want you to learn through your audition experience yesterday?"

"Not to be stupid, I guess." She tried to be nonchalant, wanting to put it behind her like a bad dream.

The enthusiastic adversary chose various ways to vilify his vague, ethereal foe.

"Not to set yourself up as your own standard."

Abi thought this through as she crunched her Grape-Nuts and finished scribbling out her spelling homework. She smashed all ten words into two sentences—a record, even for Abi Crim, spelling genius.

"Botany," said the truncated man, "is an alternate and mountainous science."

"Tuning to your own A string is like doing a paper and saying it should be an A paper just because you did it, whether or not it meets the teacher's standards."

"I guess you're right, Mom," Abi said. She scraped the bottom of her bowl for one last crunchy cereal bit, then slipped her folded spelling paper into her notebook.

5 Grandma

Dear Grandma, (Abi wrote)

Two days in a row have been humiliating. I had to stay in at recess to talk to my teacher. Mrs. Cotton said my spelling homework was not up to par. What is par*? She wouldn't let me do it during lunch to get it over with. I have to do it again tonight!*

And also, I have to sit in the second violins. This is the worst thing that has ever happened to me. My audition WAS bad, but I can't believe I am not even in the first violin section. It is very humiliating. Some fifth graders are in the first section, and I am the only sixth grader in the seconds. Maybe I will quit orchestra.

Love, Abi

P.S. I did get an invitation to a party today.

Abi clicked the send button on the computer, then closed down the e-mail program and opened up a word-processing file. She stared at the blank screen for a long time, Mrs. Cotton's speech rolling through her brain.

"Abigail," Mrs. Cotton had said, laser-beaming her with her fabulous dark eyes, "I do not know what to make of this." She said the *this* as if she were personally offended by Abi's work.

"Oh," Abi said.

"What *is* it?" Mrs. Cotton said, pointing down at Abi's two spelling sentences, which looked shriveled and lost on the page.

"My spelling homework."

Mrs. Cotton held up the page and read aloud:

The enthusiastic adversary chose various ways to vilify his vague, ethereal foe. "Botany," said the truncated man, "is an alternate and mountainous science."

Abi hung her head, realizing that it was absurd to turn in such an assignment to Mrs. Cotton. *How could I have thought that was worth turning in at all?*

"Is this the best work you can do?"

She shook her head no.

"I require a spoken response."

"No, ma'am." Her voice was hushed.

"I thought not. Take it home. Do it again. Five points off."

"Yes, ma'am." And Abi had slunk out the door to her vague, truncated recess, wondering whether Mr. Doyle's father was feeling any better.

That night, at home, after writing e-mail to Grandma Johnson, Abi typed her name and the date at the top of the page, then listed the spelling words.

Okay, she thought, do it right, Crim. She bit her lip, steadied her mind, and began to type. Five minutes later, smiling and relieved, she clicked on file, chose print, adjusted the graphics to print a low-resolution—Dad said don't waste ink—and printed her new page.

During dinner the phone rang. Dad flinched, but Will ran to get it.

"Hi, Grandma!" he said, his voice happy and surprised. Grandma never called. She used e-mail. She said e-mail was her lifeline, and if she wanted to talk to someone out loud, well, she had her dog Ludwig and her neighbor Elsa. "Sure," Will said, "I'll tell her. Bye!"

"That was Grandma," Will said. "She wants Abi to check her e-mail." He turned to her and grinned. "She said, 'What's that girl doing when she should be reading her mail?'"

Abi jumped up, but Mom said, "After dinner, Abi. One thing at a time."

Dinner talk was bits and pieces of everyone's lives. Dad felt better today. He didn't talk about Baby Betsy, but he did mention a new baby with a heart problem and told them that one of the young nurses was getting married.

Will talked about the high school orchestra and soccer and a new girl named Annie who sat by him in three classes, played the cello, and had the longest hair he'd ever seen. "Past her knees," he said. "I wonder if she ever gets tangled up in it." He did an imitation of a person trying to escape long entangling hair, complete with shrieks and gaspings for breath. "Help me!"

"Will," Mom said. "Enough."

Will coughed and straightened himself up in his chair.

"Did orchestra go any better today, Punkin?" Dad asked.

"Yeah," said Will. "Did Mrs. Denim put you where you belong?"

Abi slammed her fork down by her plate. "Her name is Mrs. Cotton, Will. Not linen, or polyester, or denim. It's cotton, okay, and she put me in the second violins, if you want to know."

"Sorry," Will said. "I didn't mean anything by it. I like cotton. Cotton is good. This shirt I'm wearing? One hundred percent cotton."

"Tell the whole story, Abi," Mom said. "More rice, Mark? Will? Abi?" She took more rice for herself and passed the dish around.

"I'm first chair of the second violins."

"Oh," Dad said, "congratulations."

"It's terrible, Dad," she said, her voice rising. "Last year I was fourth in the first violins, and now I've been demoted to the seconds."

"Abigail, say 'thank-you' when someone congratulates you." Mom's voice was firm.

"Thank you, Dad."

"And you were not demoted," Mom went on, hammering Abi flat with her quiet voice. "Mrs. Cotton seated you in the spot you earned."

"Yes, ma'am," she said, knowing Mom was right, wishing she were wrong and that it was Mrs. Cotton's fault, not hers, that she was placed so low.

"Who made concertmaster?" Will asked.

"Tamika Mitchell. She's new this year. She's the concertmistress," Abi said. "Mrs. Cotton said we women should not be afraid of feminine distinctives."

Dad laughed. "I like this Mrs. Cotton more and more."

Abi turned to look at Dad, wondering what he meant.

"She's making you think," he said. "Glad we were able to snag her. She wasn't easy to get. Especially in the middle of the night just hours before the start of school. It was a miracle, really."

"Jerry Walters says you took her because you were desperate."

Dad's face grew dark. "We *were* desperate," he said, "but that doesn't make the fact that Iris Cotton agreed to teach for us anything less than astounding."

Abi studied her plate. She wondered if she should mention the other thing Jerry had said that day.

"Jerry also said that Mrs. Cotton chose Tamika for concertmistress because she was black."

Dad put his fork down and wiped his mouth.

"What exactly did Jerry say?" he said.

Abi's stomach felt funny. She bit her lip. "Well, a whole bunch of us were talking at recess, and Jerry came up to us and said—"

"Yes?"

"He said, 'Nice going, Tamika. Good thing you're black, isn't it? That's why she picked you for concert manager, you know.' "

"What happened then?" Will asked.

Abi breathed deeply. "A few kids laughed because Jerry had said concert manager instead of concertmistress."

"I don't suppose Tamika laughed," Mom said.

"No, she walked away."

"And you?" Dad said. "What did Abi Crim do?"

Abi sat paralyzed. Her fork clattered to her plate. She stared at Dad and blinked hard. With sudden clarity a recently memorized Bible verse came to her mind: *Therefore to him that knoweth to do good, and doeth it not, to him it is sin.*

"Abigail Jane," Dad said, "do you mean to imply that you said nothing to Jerry? That you let Tamika walk away alone after that disgusting display of racism?"

"I'm sorry." Her voice trembled. Her eyes burned.

Dad leaned back in his chair. He looked at Abi for a long moment, then spoke: "Go to your room."

She flung herself on her bed and sobbed. Ten minutes passed. Then the door opened and Dad entered.

"Get your shoes on, Punkin. Get in the car."

Dad backed the car out of the driveway in silence. Abi had the feeling that Dad was going to drive her to the police station and turn her in.

"This child," she imagined him saying, "is a disgrace to society. She didn't stand up for a friend."

"Where are we going?"

"A couple of places," he said. "You have some apologizing to do, Punkin, don't you?"

She hung her head. "Yes, sir."

Tamika's house stood at the end of a cul-de-sac, in solitary splendor, rising up tall to three storeys, with dormer windows looking out like eyes.

The door opened.

"Dr. Mitchell?" Abi's father said. "I'm Mark Crim. I appreciate your allowing us to intrude upon you like this. I felt it was important for Abi's sake."

"It's nice to meet you, Mark," Dr. Mitchell said, extending his hand. "And you must be Abi."

"Hello," Abi said, wondering if she should shake his hand. He patted her back instead. "I'll get Tam."

"What is it, Papa?" she heard Tamika say. When Tamika entered the living room, Abi stood up.

"Abi! What are you doing here?"

"Hi," Abi said. "You have a nice house."

"Mark," said Dr. Mitchell, "let me show you my aquariums. I have just acquired the most interesting specimen for my new saltwater tank."

Abi guessed by Tamika's inquiring face that her father had not told her why they had come.

"What's up?" she said.

"I need to apologize to you," Abi said. "Today when Jerry made that rude comment about you, I didn't stick up for you. I'm really sorry."

"Thanks, Abi," Tamika said. "It wasn't the nicest thing anyone has ever said to me, that's for sure."

The girls looked at each other for a few seconds. Then, Tamika smiled.

"Come here," she said, "I want to show you something." She grabbed Abi's arm and pulled her into her room.

"Look at this . . . " Rifling through her top drawer, she pulled out a concert program. "I got this when we went to New York City in July. See?" Tamika pointed. Abi stared and grabbed for the program.

"How did you get this?"

Tamika laughed. "I knew you would appreciate it because you're such a good violinist. I wanted it so badly; Mom said if I wanted it, I could get it, but I had to want it badly enough to go backstage by myself."

"Wow," Abi said, running her finger over the signature: *Pinchas Zukerman.* "You're amazing."

"I almost died of fright," she said, and laughed.

She said I was such a good violinist.

The ride to Jerry's house seemed longer to Abi. Her mouth was dry. She tried to think through how she would apologize to him. When his mother opened the front door, Abi's hands trembled. *This is scarier than Tamika's. At least Tamika is nice!*

"Butch, they're here."

Jerry slunk into the room like a whipped dog and flung himself down onto the couch.

"What?" he said, impatiently, like Abi and her father were an intrusion on his otherwise interesting evening. His attitude enraged Abi, and she had the sudden urge to spit on him or slap him. Dad must have felt this.

"Abi," he said. "Speak."

"I should have corrected you today," she said, "when you said what you said about Mrs. Cotton and Tamika. I am sorry. I don't agree with you."

"What?" he said, like she had slapped him and he didn't know why.

"Tamika got concertmistress because she played better than anybody else. That's why."

"Whatever," said Jerry.

Later, while Dad and Abi were licking ice-cream cones at Nona's Ice Cream Shoppe, Abi laughed.

"That's the scariest thing I've ever had to do," she said.

"You did great, Punkin. I'm proud of you."

She smiled. In less than an hour, she had gone from being a disgrace to her family to being someone her dad was proud of.

"Thanks, Dad."

When they got home, there was another telephone message from Grandma.

"She says, 'Baby, get on that computer,' " Will said, laughing. "I can't believe she called twice. She must be sitting by her computer waiting for you to write her back!"

Abi logged on and pulled up the e-mail.

Abi, Baby—(it read)

What a hoot! Playing all the wrong notes—that'll teach you, sweetie-pie! Ha ha. Well, you get to sit second violins. Better than viola, no? Ha ha, just kidding. Take up the oboe, and you'll be first chair automatically. Nobody plays oboe. Or maybe bassoon. Your grandpa played bassoon, but he died, so maybe you should stick with violin.

Quit orchestra? What a laugh! Ridiculous! Absurd!

What is par? Par is hitting the golf ball into the hole in the number of strokes the course manager thinks it should take you, which is usually something like four or five, but basically, when I play golf, I take as many strokes as I need, which is many, many, many more than "par," but I don't quit playing golf because what else is there to do in this town anyway, except shuffleboard?

Now, the reason I am writing is this: Elsa came over here tonight, and she had a wonderful idea. "Vada," she said to me, "are you going to see your kids this year again?" And I said, of course, because I'm planning to come at Thanksgiving like always. I'll stay a week or two. What's an RV for if not to drive out to see my family? So then Elsa said to me, "Melba's granddaughter flew out to see her and then drove back with her when she went to their home."

Well, baby, what about it? I'm planning to come for Thanksgiving, like I said. You come back with me when your school gets out for Christmas vacation! Then you can fly home—alone!—in time for school to start up again in January. Ask your Dad. Ask your Mom. What do you think?

Love, Grandma

P.S. I will pay half your airfare home if you can come.

P.P.S. Have fun at the party. But don't do anything stupid. Always call home if the party gets stupid. YOU KNOW what I mean.

Abi printed out the letter and read it again. She ran her finger over the part about Grandpa.

Grandpa's bassoon. Grandpa's music. Playing violin reminds me of him.

She read through the rest of the letter, laughing at the P.S. and the YOU KNOW, as if anyone at a sixth-grade party would do anything bad.

She liked the idea of going home with Grandma at Christmastime and then flying back alone. It would be fun to drive to Parkerton with Grandma, but sad to miss Christmas with the family in Fairlawn. The idea of flying home alone sounded scary and exciting all at once.

She showed the letter to Mom and then wrote Grandma back.

Dear Grandma, (she wrote)

I will come if Mom lets me. It scares me to think about flying alone, but my new friend Tamika went backstage at a concert and got Pinchas Zukerman's autograph, and if she can do that, maybe I can fly solo. Thank you for writing to me. It is late, and we are having devotions now. Bye bye.

Love, Abi

P.S. There will not be any drugs at the party.

P.P.S. Of course.

6 Person of the Week

"Abigail, I'd like to see you."

"Yes, ma'am." As the class filed out for recess, Abi was left with a thudding in her heart. Her hands sweated, and she felt her face redden as the room emptied. She looked around the classroom as the minutes ticked by, wondering if she should remind Mrs. Cotton she was there.

Though only a few days had passed since the first day of school, the room had been transformed from Mr. Doyle's domain to Mrs. Cotton's kingdom. Down were the maps tacked to bulletin boards with white paper backing, and up were the Question Boards backed with star-spangled wrapping paper, challenging the students with questions in large red letters that inquired: *How do you know that God loves you?* or *How do you know that America is free?* Student papers answering the questions were tacked to the board, and Mrs. Cotton encouraged her students to reply to the opinion papers in writing, whether they agreed or disagreed.

Another thing Mrs. Cotton had done was to take down the discolored window blinds.

"I don't like those things," she'd said. "Besides, how can we see outside if the windows are blocked? Don't you sometimes ache to go outside?"

Abi looked out those windows now, aching as she watched her classmates on the playground, while Mrs. Cotton finished writing on the board. Finally, she turned and walked toward Abi. She stopped at Tamika's desk and sat down. Mrs. Cotton was holding a paper.

"Well, Abi," she said, laying the paper on Abi's desk, smoothing it out. It was the revised spelling-sentence paper, the one Abi had done on the computer the night of Grandma Johnson's e-mail frenzy.

"Yes, ma'am." Mrs. Cotton always required a spoken answer.

"It's much better than the first time."

Abi smiled, relieved. "Thank you," she said. Now everything would be back to normal. She knew how to get on Mrs. Cotton's good side, at least in spelling-land.

"Much better," Mrs. Cotton said, smiling. She took her red pen and marked a large C on the top of the page. Abi gasped.

"A *C?*" Abi had never had a C before in her whole life. Her mouth fell open. Her eyes teared up.

"Yes," Mrs. Cotton said. "This is right up to average now. Well done."

Abi sat dumbfounded. This was not what she had expected at all. She had expected congratulations on her brilliant revision. She'd expected the paper to be put up on the Snoopy-papered *Good Work!* board.

"Well, here you go, Abigail," Mrs. Cotton said. "You may go out to your recess now."

"Thank you," Abi whispered, and took the paper from her hand.

That afternoon, Mrs. Cotton was not in class. Instead, a substitute teacher, Mrs. Baumble, rapped her knuckles on the lectern.

"The class will come to attention," said Mrs. Baumble.

"Yes, ma'am," the students said, mindful that Mrs. Cotton always required a spoken answer.

"Please do not speak unless I ask you to," said Mrs. Baumble. Mrs. Baumble's stern expression permeated the room with something between fear and sadness. No one knew what to do. No one spoke.

"Your teacher," she said, "is gone for the afternoon. I do not know where, nor do I think it is any of my business. Or, frankly, your business. However, to set your minds at rest, I do not think she is ill."

An audible sigh of relief spilled over the room.

"As I am not in the habit of teaching—in fact, I have never taught a day of school in my life—I shall not attempt it here. Shall we say the school does not have the longest list of substitute teachers from which to draw?"

Abi looked around the room for any sign of comfort and found none. All the other students wore looks of disgust or frustration.

"So, since your teacher is otherwise engaged for the afternoon—and mind, it is not up to us to cast aspersions on her plans for the day, knowing as she did that she had a class to teach—no, it is just our concern to take care of matters here where we find ourselves. That is, in this room. Now, as I do not wish to begin a teaching career at this time of my life—watch that smirk, young man—please take a reading book out of your desk and read until dismissal time."

Groans crossed the room. Abi reached into her desk and found *The Prince and the Pauper.* She was glad to have checked this out last time she was at the school library. At least it would hold her attention through the next two hours.

She looked around the room. Mindy had a Little House book. Tamika was studying her music, tapping her fingers lightly on her desk, moving them as if with vibrato. Jerry made a pile of his textbooks on his desk and paged through them, leaf by leaf, picking his nose and saying quietly, "Is that so?" and "You don't say?" time after time.

By the time the three o'clock bell rang, Abi felt drained. Twain would be better, she thought, if she could read him while prone on her bed, with a CD of Mozart playing. Reading for two hours while sitting up straight in a school chair could ruin even the greatest book.

Orchestra was canceled for the afternoon. She was glad. If there was one thing in the world that would be more awful than class with Mrs. Baumble it would be orchestra with Mrs. Baumble. She liked the way Mrs. Cotton held her baton. And the way she said, "Instruments up." And the way she had told Abi she would be principal second violin.

"Let's just say," Mrs. Cotton had said, "that your audition was unfortunate. However, your technique is advanced, and frankly, Abi, I need your leadership in the seconds."

Mrs. Cotton had taken her failure and turned it into responsibility.

However, today, with the spelling fiasco—a C!—fresh in her mind, Abi needed to get home. She needed to spill her offended feelings out on e-mail to Grandma in all caps, flaming her with her disappointment.

Kimberly was waiting for her on her front porch, swaying in the Crims' porch swing. A mug of steaming cocoa sat on the railing.

"How was school?"

"Just a second. Let me put my things inside." Back outside, Abi settled into the swing next to Kimberly.

"So?" Kimberly said. "How was your day? Tell me everything."

"I got a C," she said. She hadn't wanted to tell Kimberly this, but the words spurted out.

"You didn't!"

"I did. On spelling."

Kimberly looked sideways at her from her place on the swing.

"You got a C on a spelling test? This I will not believe, Miss Straight-A's-Since-Kindergarten, Miss Spelling Champion of Fairlawn Christian School."

"It wasn't a spelling test," Abi said. "It was a paper. You know, 'Use ten of your spelling words in a sentence,' that kind of paper."

"I wish I had that kind of paper. Mom makes me write my words out ten times each!"

"That would have been easier, believe me."

"Well, let me see your paper."

Abi ran into the house and got the paper, then unfolded it and handed it to Kimberly, who read aloud:

"I was enthusiastic when I met my adversary in the way. He had various weapons to vilify me with. I had a vague and ethereal fear of the mountainous way and the alternate, truncated path that led through the botanical woods."

"Hmm," said Kimberly. "It's interesting."

"Do you think it's only a C paper?" Abi asked, worried.

"Who cares what I think?" she said. "Your teacher thinks it's a C, so it's a C."

Kimberly handed the paper back with a smile, and the conversation turned to her day of home schooling.

"We watched a science video, and then I had to do the experiment in the kitchen," Kimberly said. "I'm always afraid things will blow up, but nothing did. Then we went to the art museum and I sketched a couple of the paintings, but they didn't turn out very well."

Kimberly stayed until Mom poked her head out the door and said, "Time to set the table."

"See you tomorrow," Kimberly said, and then, "You could get an A on that paper if you wanted to." She skipped down the steps, waving good-bye.

"Today I weighed one hundred sixty-two and a half pounds," Mom said, staring down at roasted chicken without skin, rice without salt or butter, and her steamed vegetable. "It's just the way I am, I guess. Four generations of fat, and what can you do?"

"You're not fat," Dad said.

"Moms should be soft," Will said.

"I got a C today," Abi said.

"A C?" everyone said. Three pairs of eyes locked on to her face. She blushed.

"Mrs. Cotton didn't like my spelling homework."

"Again?" Will said. "I thought you revised it. Who does this Mrs. Rayon think she is, anyway?"

"Yes, I did revise it," she said, feeling that if Will would take her side, everything would be fine, thinking that maybe his fabric names for her teacher weren't all that bad after all.

"What was wrong with it?" Dad asked.

"I don't know," she said. "She said it was average work and deserved an average grade."

"Perhaps," said Will, "the woman, the esteemed Mrs. Leather, does not know you are a straight-A student."

"Yeah," Abi said, feeling avenged. Maybe if Mrs. Cotton were told about her long-standing record of good grades, she would let this slide, so it wouldn't affect her report-card grade.

"Maybe," said Dad, "you didn't work up to Mrs. Cotton's—Will, her name is Mrs. Cotton—standard of excellence."

"Yes," said Mom. "That's true." Mom took a long drink of iced tea. "You know, Abi, this might just be another case of your settling for your own accustomed level."

Abi hung her head. "Like tuning to my own A string?"

Mom and Dad nodded and turned the conversation to other, less important things, like taxes and the presidential race, and the short work force in the neonatal nursery. Suddenly Dad turned to her. "How was your substitute today, Punkin?"

"Oh, Mrs. Baumble. She's mean. Made us read for two solid hours. We weren't allowed to get up for any reason. Some kids had to read their textbooks because they weren't allowed to go to the bookshelf."

Dad laughed, but Abi did not see anything funny. "It's the bane of my life, having to find substitute teachers for that school. We were absolutely out of subs today. I called Mrs. Baumble on a hunch that she might not have anything of importance to do today. She seemed quite pleased at the request."

"She didn't seem pleased in the classroom," Abi said.

The dinner talk wafted over her as she wondered whether she'd get a C every week and whether Mrs. Cotton would ease up on her. Who did Mrs. Cotton think she was, anyway, to put her in the second violins when she was obviously first-violin material, and give her C's on her homework assignments? After all, she was only the fill-in teacher when the real teacher, Mr. Doyle, couldn't make it because his father . . .

"Abi," Dad's voice cracked her daydream. "The phone, Punkin."

She picked up the receiver. "Hello," she said. "Hi, Tamika. What's up?"

Then, "What?" and "You're kidding?" and "Thanks, I'll run to Kimberly's."

She slammed the phone down and whirled around.

"I'll be right back," she said. "It's sort of an emergency," and ran out the door.

A minute later she was sitting on Kimberly's floor, her eyes glued to the television. Mrs. Edison had been shocked, no doubt, by her frantic banging on their front door and her insistent, "I need to see the news!"

The Crims did not have a television. Dad believed that television was an evil plot to turn good American citizens into "automatons" and "secular humanists." Mom agreed. Besides, she liked having a quiet, peaceful house.

Kimberly and Abi sat on the floor. The dog, Ferdinand, sat in front of them, chewing on a rag doll and flopping his tail on the floor, whap, whap.

"Thank you, Mort," said the television newsman. "And now, for our regular Thursday feature, Person of the Week, we'll go to Linda Meierbaum at the Phipps Center. Linda?"

"Thank you, John," said Linda Meierbaum, a flashy newslady whose hair blew behind her as the camera closed in. "Behind me you see the Phipps Center, where young people with disadvantaged backgrounds come to learn life skills in a safe, encouraging environment."

The camera focused on a group of kids behind Ms. Meierbaum. They were playing basketball.

"Our Person of the Week is the founder and director of the Phipps Center of Musical Arts, Mrs. Iris Cotton. I spoke with Iris this afternoon in the center auditorium."

Abi gasped and grabbed Kimberly's arm as the picture changed. Now inside the Phipps Center auditorium, Linda Meierbaum sat across from Mrs. Cotton, who was resplendent in the bright African-print dress she'd worn to school that morning. Her gold earrings flashed. Her smile lit the television.

"That's my teacher," she said.

"That's your Mrs. Cotton?" Kimberly said.

"Yeah."

"Wow."

"Mrs. Cotton, tell us what you do here at the Phipps Center and why you believe your work is important?" Linda Meierbaum's voice was deep and searching.

"I work with a group of instrumentalists who would otherwise not have access to a symphony experience," Mrs. Cotton said. She sounded confident, assured. "Many of our kids come from impoverished homes, where there is no money for instruments or lessons. We take the kids and train them."

"We?"

"My husband and I. We give lessons on Saturdays and then rehearse the orchestra on Thursday and Friday nights."

"You volunteer your time for the lessons, I understand," Ms. Meierbaum said, "but what about the instruments?"

Mrs. Cotton grinned. "I beg for them," she said. "We ask businesses to donate money and instruments. Many people have old instruments they don't use anymore. And many businesspeople are uncomfortable turning me down when I ask for money. I lay the cause on very thick." She laughed a soft, silvery laugh.

"Tell me what inspired you to begin this orchestra," Ms. Meierbaum said.

"Well," Mrs. Cotton looked directly into the camera, and Abi caught the note of urgency and challenge in her voice, "as a citizen, I wanted to do something to contribute to my community. As a child from a poor black family, I had a difficult beginning. But I got to college and graduated. I knew then that if I could work hard and become a teacher and a trained musician, some of these kids could too. If only they were given a chance. My husband and I decided we would be the ones to provide the chance. To make a difference in the lives of some kids."

Mrs. Cotton's eyes flashed. She continued.

"And, as a Christian, I view this work as a ministry—a way to get to know these kids so I can share the love of Christ and the message of the gospel with them."

"That's interesting," said Ms. Meierbaum. "Tell us, Iris, how well do your budding musicians play?"

Mrs. Cotton laughed. "Maybe it would be better if you heard them."

The camera angle changed and zoomed in on the orchestra, waiting quietly for their moment of TV stardom. Mrs. Cotton strode to the conductor's music stand, raised her arms for the "instruments up" signal, tapped out a measure, and hit the downbeat.

Strains of Mozart filled the air. Abi sat back on her heels and sighed. So that was why the class had had a substitute this afternoon. Mrs. Cotton had to do her civic duty and become the Channel 7 Person of the Week. Abi loved her as she watched the way the kids played for her, and she wanted to practice hard and play well so she could be worthy of being in her orchestra.

Then, the camera backed off. They were back outside with Linda Meierbaum live.

"Well, John, that was the Phipps Center orchestra under the direction of our Person of the Week, Mrs. Iris Cotton. She does a wonderful job with those kids."

"She sure does, Linda. She certainly spends a good deal of her time helping children."

"Yes, John, she does. In fact, I learned that in her spare time she teaches sixth grade at Fairlawn Christian School."

"Well," John said, "our Person of the Week is quite a lady."

"That she is, John. Now back to you."

"Thank you, Linda."

Kimberly switched off the television. She sat back down beside Abi on the floor and scratched Ferdinand's head. A clock chimed the quarter-hour in the hall.

"That's the Mrs. Cotton who says you're average?" Kimberly said.

"Yeah."

"You need to crank up your work, Abi," Kimberly said. "She's awesome."

"I know."

Two hours later, the revised-revised spelling paper was finished. It was a full page of a Cotton-inspired story. Abi wouldn't get a grade on it, she knew, but it didn't matter. If Mrs. Cotton could spend every day of her life helping people, leading orchestras, giving lessons, then Abi could work up a decent spelling story for her.

Afterwards she e-mailed Grandma, attaching her homework file to the end.

Dear Grandma, (she wrote)

My teacher was on the news! Tamika called to tell me, and I had to run to Kimberly's so fast I almost fell over the curb. My teacher is awesome. She was Person of the Week. I did this paper (attached) for her. Do you like it?

The party is tomorrow night. I can't wait.

Maybe Christmas at your house!

Love, Abi

She was full of talk about Mrs. Cotton all night. When Mom cuddled with her that night, Abi told her about her resolution.

"I'm going to work really hard to measure up to Mrs. Cotton's standard instead of my own. I'm going to try to please her, not just get the work done."

"Good job, Abi," Mom said. "I'm proud of you."

In the morning when Abi stumbled out into the hall, rubbing her eyes, Mom came bounding down the hall toward her, wearing yellow sweatpants and a pink sweatshirt. She was huffing and sweating.

"What—"

"I've been jogging," she said. "Got up at dawn."

"Why?"

"I decided not to settle down under four generations of fat. I'm going to get going and work to a higher standard."

Abi smiled, sleepily proud of Mom.

"If you can write stellar spelling papers," she said, "I can get my old body moving."

At breakfast that morning, Mom announced that she would be forming a walking club that day.

"I am going to tell the girls that the days of excuses are over. We are going to meet a higher standard of physical excellence. We are going to tackle our own forty-year-old realities. We are not going to settle for flapping arms and bouncing bellies—"

"Please, Ellen," said Dad, "we're eating."

"No more trembling tummies," Mom said.

"Ellen!"

"Sorry."

"Pass the butter, please," said Will, "if that's okay."

Mom passed him the butter. "Never in my adult life," she said, "have I gotten below one hundred and fifty pounds. I'm here to state that I'm going to meet that challenge and then some. I am going to meet the higher standard. Or the lower, if you get what I mean."

"You've said it three times now, dear."

"Meet the higher standard," Mom said.

7 The Party

Mom opened her eye wide and leaned forward on her elbow, getting close to the mirror.

"I always put my mascara on first," she said. "That way, if I smudge it up real badly, I don't have to do my whole face over again."

Mom carefully brushed the mascara onto her eyelashes, like an artist. She was getting ready to go out with Dad, and Abi was watching her, hoping it wouldn't be too long before she would be allowed to wear makeup of her own. Mom crimped her eyelashes with the eyelash curler. It seemed primitive and strange to Abi, squeezing an eyelash like that, so she looked away, down to Mom's pictures arranged in clumps, like a family reunion on her dressing table. Mom had told her about all the pictures many times.

"Tell me again about Great Aunt Mabel," Abi said. She pointed to a faded photograph in a gold frame worked with flowers.

"That's Great Aunt Mabel's high school graduation picture," she said. "See how they tinted the lips sort of pinkish? That was in the late forties, I think, before color photography was common."

Abi picked up the picture frame and tried to remember what Great Aunt Mabel had looked like before she died, and wondered how such an old lady could have looked as beautiful as the teenaged girl looking out from the picture.

"You have her eyes," Mom said. She tipped her bottle of foundation over onto her finger to get a little, then smoothed it over her forehead and rubbed it in evenly.

Abi stood behind Mom while she sat on her little chair, her makeup and hairbrushes before her. The photographs—old ones like Aunt Mabel and new ones like last year's school pictures—stared back at her, some happy, some serious.

"This is my favorite picture," Abi said. She picked up the picture of Mom and Dad on their wedding day. Mom was smiling a happily-ever-aftering kind of smile, and Dad looked happy and strong. "I love your dress, Mom."

"I saved it for you," said Mom. She was patting her face all over with powder. "To set the foundation," she said.

"Where is the dress?"

"In my closet. I'll show you sometime."

Mom opened her blush compact and surveyed her face. Abi moved a little closer to Mom. When she looked down, she noticed that Mom's dresser drawer was open and something golden was lying on the bottom of the drawer. It was a locket. Abi wondered if there was a picture in it. She picked it up and opened it.

"Who's this baby?" Abi asked.

Mom glanced up, and stiffened.

"Give me that, please." Mom spoke softly, and Abi handed the locket to her. Mom cradled it in her hand and stared at it.

"Is it me?"

"No." Mom's voice was soft and faraway. "This is Marigold. She was my first baby."

"Oh," Abi said. "I thought Will . . ."

"She was the most beautiful baby there ever was," Mom said. "Her eyes were sky blue, and her skin was the sweetest pink."

Mom touched the miniature face and fingered the oval frame.

"She lived three days."

"Oh, sorry, Mom," Abi said. "I didn't know."

"That's why Dad does what he does," she said. "Because of Marigold."

Abi tiptoed out of the room and shut the door softly behind her. She heard Will tune his cello in his room, then draw a long, deep minor scale like sorrow filling the house.

Dad was sitting at the kitchen table, leaning over the newspaper with a pencil in his hand. He was already dressed to go out to dinner.

"Hi, Dad."

"Hi, Punkin. What's a five-letter word for 'computer dragger'?"

"Mouse," Abi said. "Mom told me about Marigold."

Dad's head snapped up. "Is she okay?"

Abi didn't say anything. Dad jumped up and jogged down the hall. He tapped the door gently. "You okay?" Abi heard him say before he disappeared behind the bedroom door.

A few minutes later Mom came out. She was dressed up, but Abi noticed that she didn't have any makeup on. She and Dad had a cup of coffee and talked quietly while Abi waited by the front door with her sleeping bag and backpack full of sleepover things.

Then Mom went back to do her face again. She didn't invite Abi to watch this time. Instead, Dad sat with her on the couch and told her about Marigold.

"I married your mother after she graduated from college. I'd put four years into the army and was ready to settle down. Everything was wonderful for us," Dad said. "We were twenty-three years old, with our whole lives ahead of us. We had a nice apartment and good jobs. I sold cars at the Ford dealership, and Mom taught a fifth-grade class at the Christian school. When we found out several months later that Mom was going to have a baby, we were very excited. It made everything perfect."

Dad put his arm around Abi and hugged her close.

"Our baby was supposed to arrive in December, so we called her our 'Christmas Baby' all that spring and summer."

Will's minor scales faded into the Brahms's lullaby melody, resonating. The low tones of the cello melded with the sadness in Dad's voice.

"But our Christmas baby came in August," Dad said. "It was too soon. She held on for three days, struggling to live. Then, when it became clear she would not be able to live . . ." Dad paused, swallowed. "We were able to get her disconnected from the machines. Mom held her while she died.

"Mom rocked her and sang 'Jesus Loves Me' over her. Our pastor came and prayed with us, committing our precious

Marigold to God. Then we handed our little girl back to her nurse and left the hospital. It was the hardest thing we've ever had to do.

"Marigold was buried in a white lace dress your mother had worn as a baby. I tucked my own teddy bear, that I'd had since I was a little boy, into the little coffin with her. Our whole world had ended. It was like the light went out for a long, long time.

"After that I went to nursing school so I could help other people who were in similar situations. Many of my friends thought it was strange that I should be a nurse, being a man, but it was something I felt God had prepared me to do. And I have never regretted the decision.

"After I finished school, we moved out here for this job, so I could help little babies like Marigold. Over the years, the pain of losing her lessened. But sometimes, when we visit Grandma in Parkerton, Mom and I go to the cemetery there, to put flowers on Marigold's grave."

The deep tones of Will's cello practice filled the whole house like mourning.

"Dad," she said, "how come you never told me this?" She thought, but didn't say, that she was almost twelve years old now and should know things like this. That she had once had a sister.

"Mom keeps it in her heart. It is our private grief."

"Is it a secret?"

"No, it's not a secret, but it is private."

"Does Will know?"

"Yes, Will knows. And the rest of the family. And many of our friends from back home where it happened. But out here we don't talk about it unless Mom brings it up."

Dad smiled and messed up Abi's hair with his heavy hand. "Talking about Marigold makes Mom cry," he said, smiling. "And then she has to do her makeup again and make us late for our dinner reservations."

In the car, on the way to Mindy's house, Abi breathed in Mom's "going out" perfume and counted years. Mom was forty-one years old. So, if she'd had her big sister Marigold when she was twenty-three—and if Marigold had lived—Abi would have an eighteen-year-old sister now. She sighed aloud and wondered what it would be like to have a grown-up sister.

The car stopped. She could see some of her friends playing in the back yard. She opened her door, but Dad's voice stopped her.

"What's the Crim party rule, Punkin?"

"Call home at any time if there's something bad going on."

"Okey dokey, kiddo," Dad said. He smiled and winked at her. "You've got it. Now get on in there and have a good time."

Abi waved as the car drove off, and Mom called, "Have fun, Honey. We'll pick you up in the morning." Then Abi turned and marched toward the house, her sleeping bag swinging beside her.

Time to be the life of the party at the first party of the year.

Mindy showed her where to leave her things, and then Abi joined the other girls in the back yard. Jennifer was there, and Kristy. Jessica and Amy. Other girls from class and a couple of girls from Mindy's neighborhood arrived. Soon a large group of girls were chomping potato chips and giggling in the back yard.

Mindy's mother, Mrs. Rossman, could be seen through the kitchen window. She was frosting a cake. Mr. Rossman was on the deck, barbecuing hot dogs.

The Rossmans had a full acre of mown lawn to run around, and within minutes all the girls were screaming, throwing Katie's stolen shoe around, while Katie ran from one side of the yard to the other shouting, "Give me my shoe, already," and "Hey, no fair; give it back."

Abi stuffed down three hot dogs and half a plate of potato chips, and then devoured a huge slice of Mrs. Rossman's famous chocolate-frosted chocolate layer cake, topped with chocolate ice cream, dripping with chocolate syrup.

The girls talked and laughed until ten-thirty when Mr. and Mrs. Rossman went upstairs. Then they gathered in the kitchen to drink soda pop and eat cookies.

"What'd you guys think of that Mrs. Baumble?" Jennifer said. Jennifer had the coveted classroom position of back corner seat closest to the window.

"What a loser," Mindy said, pouring herself another glass of soda pop and belching like a boy. "She's the worst! I hope she never ever darkens our classroom door again."

"That's for sure," said Kristy. "In fact, I hope we never have another sub. My dad says the school should do something about getting good subs, especially since Mr. Doyle had to leave. It's like Mrs. Cotton is a sub, and then old Mrs. Baumble was the sub for the sub."

"Mrs. Cotton is not a sub," Abi said. "She's our teacher."

"You only say that because your dad's on the school board," Katie said. Abi felt helpless and undefended. She vowed she would stand up for Mrs. Cotton no matter what happened.

"Subs are the worst," said Amber, one of Mindy's neighborhood friends. "We had one at our school named Mrs. Plather. She was pathetic, let me tell you. She made us stand up whenever she called on us. One boy wouldn't stand up, and old Plather made him go to the office."

Abi sipped her soda pop, feeling uneasy. It wasn't drugs or drinking, but this kind of talk wasn't right either.

"Time for Truth or Dare," Mindy said, jumping up and stretching. "We've got to get this party going. I'll start."

She walked around the room, looking at each girl, as if mulling over whom to choose for her first victim.

"Amy," she said, "you first."

"Sorry," said Amy. "I can't play."

"What's that supposed to mean, you can't play? Anyone can play Truth or Dare. You just choose whether you want to tell the truth about something or take a dare."

"I mean, my parents don't let me play Truth or Dare."

"Your parents? So what, they're not here—"

"Never mind," said Kristy. "Let's just play. Amy can watch."

"Abi," Mindy said, smiling. "Truth or dare?"

She bit her lip. At a party last year, Abi had said "Dare." Mindy had told her to run around the block. It was past midnight, and Abi had been terrified the whole time she ran. "Truth," she said.

"On a scale of one to ten, how much do you like Stephen Carpenter?"

The girls burst into laughter. Abi felt her face get red. She looked around the room, pretending to be nonchalant, uncaring.

"Six," she said.

"Six," Jennifer said, as if Abi had said something very funny.

"Okay, fine," Abi said, her face hot. "Now it's my turn." She looked over at Amy and admired her for being brave and standing up for what her parents expected. Maybe in a little while, she thought, I'll quit the game and sit with her.

"Katie, truth or dare?" she said.

"Dare." Katie's eyes shone defiance.

"Okay," Abi said. "Go into the kitchen and make a tuna and peanut butter sandwich with chocolate sauce, and eat it."

Cries of "yuck" and "oh, sick" filled the air. Abi hoped the game would end soon. It didn't. She moved over by Amy and sat by her, watching the game, trying not to be involved. Jessica dared Mindy to go outside and shout the Fairlawn Christian School cheer at the top of her voice. Then Mindy made Jennifer tell the most embarrassing thing that ever happened to her.

"I threw up on John Evans during our first-grade chapel program." Everyone laughed.

"Okay, Abi," Jennifer said, "you again. Truth or dare?"

"Truth."

Jennifer smiled. "Rank the girls in our class in the order of how you like them. The first name you say will be the person you like best, and the last name will be the person you dislike most."

Abi gasped. This was worse than the last thing she'd had to confess. "I can't do that."

"Of course you can," Jennifer said, smiling. "You just have to tell the truth. You picked 'truth.' Tell the truth. You could have said 'dare,' so it's your own fault."

Jennifer looked around the room triumphantly, like she'd caught Abi in a trap too strong to get out of. Abi stared at the ground, mentally listing the girls from the sixth-grade class.

"Can I have a piece of paper?" Abi said.

Someone got her a piece of paper and a pencil. She wrote down the names of the girls in the classroom order, which was alphabetical. Then she looked up and stared around the circle at the faces of the waiting girls. Mindy, Jennifer, Katie, Kristy, Jessica, Amy. Slowly, a realization hit her as she looked at the list in her hands and then around at the girls in the room: she realized who was missing. Tamika Mitchell, Candy Wong, Li-Chiu Harris, Jillian Red Crow.

An odd, hot feeling settled in Abi's stomach and worked up into her heart. A feeling like pain and then anger.

"Mindy," Abi said, crumpling up the list of sixth-grade girls, "did you invite all the girls in our class to this party?"

Abi noticed the other girls looking around.

"Of course not," Mindy said. "Just my friends. Just us."

"Us?"

"You know what I mean, Abi," Mindy said. "Don't pretend you don't know what I mean." She was laughing, as if Abi was a silly little child coloring outside the lines. "I just wanted it to be us."

"Just us white kids?" Abi felt her voice shaking. She hoped she wouldn't cry. "Is that what you mean? Just us white kids?" Abi wanted her dad to burst through the door and rescue her.

"Get over it, Crim," Jennifer said. "It's no big deal. Mindy can invite whoever she wants to her own party."

"That's right," Mindy said, smoothing the blue flannel of her nightgown over her knees.

A flash of anger burst through Abi, bigger than any she had felt before.

"That's right," she said. "You can have anyone you want at your own party." She scrambled to her feet and walked to the telephone on the wall. She picked up the receiver. Punched seven buttons.

"What are you doing?" Mindy said. "Are you calling Tamika to tell her? It's one o'clock in the morning."

"Dad," she said. "Sorry to call you, but can you pick me up?"

Dad's voice was large and reassuring, "I'll be right there. Stand on the porch in a safe place. Make sure there's a light on."

"I have to go now," Abi said. She rolled up her sleeping bag and stuffed her things in her backpack. She didn't hear the exact words of the buzz that floated around her. Her own heart pounded loud, blocking out other sounds. Insistent, frustrated sounds. Then, someone tapped her shoulder.

"You won't tell Tamika, will you, Abi?" Mindy's voice pleaded.

Abi closed the door behind her and stood under the porch light. She felt small and insignificant, outside in the middle of the night. She leaned against the house, afraid to move away from its security.

Have I lost all my friends so Tamika wouldn't be hurt? She wasn't even there to know about it, and I'll never tell her. Did I lose everyone else for nothing?

When the car drove up, Abi ran to it. She threw her things in the back seat and then climbed into the front seat next to Dad. She tried to stifle a laugh, but it wasn't easy. Dad's hair was messed up into random kinks, and he was wearing his pajamas under his overcoat.

"Hey, don't laugh," he said. "I'm happy to rescue my damsel in distress at any time of the day or night, but I don't promise to polish my armor first." He paused. "What happened, Punkin?"

She had finished the story by the time they drove up into the driveway at home. "Did I do right, Dad?" He leaned over and kissed her head.

"Princess," he said, "you did perfectly."

"I'm proud of you, Honey," Mom said when she'd heard a sleepy version of the story. "Talk about meeting a higher standard."

Monday afternoon, when they were packing up their instruments after orchestra practice, Tamika approached Abi.

"I heard about what you did. Thanks."

"Tamika, it was awful," Abi said. "I'm sorry you even heard about it."

"I heard Saturday morning. Stuff like that gets around. Anyway, I have something for you."

She held out a small white envelope.

"The girls from my Sunday school class are getting together this Friday night at my house. When I told them what you did at that other party, they wanted to meet you. It's Friday night from six until ten. Our parents won't let us stay overnight. They think we'll get into trouble or something."

"I'll come if I can," Abi said.

Tamika smiled. "You'll be the only white girl there."

8 Mrs. Cotton's News

Abi stood in front of the *Good Work!* board, rain dripping off her clothes and hair. There was her paper, surrounded by celebrating Snoopys. *No Credit* was written in red across the top, but she didn't care. Her C would stand, but this proved she could do a good job, even with words like *ethereal*.

> *The knight stood bravely before his enthusiastic king, a vague, questioning look on his face. "What if the enemy proves ethereal?" he thought. "What if I cannot see his truncated form?"*
>
> *"What ails thee, my good knight?" said the king. "Does the adversary frighten thee?"*
>
> *"Nay, my lord," said the knight, "but I wish for an alternate plan, peradventure the mountainous terrain is too hard for me."*
>
> *"Don't vilify yourself," said the king. "You will find various ways to deal with the flora and fauna—the botany—of the region. And all will be well. Go with speed, good sir, and come again with victory!"*

THE YEAR OF ABI CRIM

"You're weird," Jerry said, reading over her shoulder.

She ignored him and sauntered to her desk. She flopped down into her chair, rejoicing over her paper getting tacked up, happy that tomorrow was another Friday, another end of the week, another party. She was sure Tamika's party was going to be a highlight of her eleven-and-a-half years.

Mrs. Cotton was late coming back from lunch that day, so the sixth graders tromped over to the fifth-grade classroom and watched a science video. It wasn't the most exciting thing Abi had ever experienced, but at least it wasn't Mrs. Baumble.

"Sorry about the crowding, kids," the teacher said. "There wasn't anyone available to take your class, but don't worry. We like you enough to sit in close quarters for a little while."

After the video, the sixth-graders went back to their classroom. Mrs. Cotton had arrived. She seemed happy and distracted, like her mind was somewhere else. Abi wondered if she'd been down at the Phipps Music Center and if she was going to be on television again that night. And if she was, if she'd tell them about it this time. Abi raised her hand. She wanted to know.

"Yes, Abi." Mrs. Cotton's voice was light and distant. Somewhere else.

"Are you going to be on television again?"

"No, not tonight." She looked around at her students as if they were people she had never seen before. Or perhaps as if they were not even there. For a long time, Mrs. Cotton said nothing. Abi began to wonder if Stephen was going to assume command of the classroom.

"I'll read to you," Mrs. Cotton said at last.

All the desk lids went up as twenty-seven sixth graders searched for paper and colored pencils or crayons. Mrs.

Cotton always allowed the students to draw while she read. "It keeps your concentration on the story," she said, and somehow it did.

When all the desks were closed and twenty-seven hands had begun to draw, Mrs. Cotton opened the after-lunch book she had been reading for the last few days. Then she stood up. She always walked around the room when she read, up and down the aisles, punctuating the air with her finger, or tossing her glorious black hair, to emphasize something in the story. She'd walk quickly if the story was quick, or stomp ponderously if something horrible was about to happen.

"Harvard Topcoat moved closer to the street corner, fingering the bread roll in his pocket," she read. "He looked over his shoulder hastily, but could see nothing through the dense fog of the dark London night."

Then she stopped, sighed, walked back to her desk, and sat down.

"I am sorry," she said, closing the book. "I am unable to read. I'll put some music on. Please continue to draw. Or else, you may read."

Mrs. Cotton sat at her desk looking out the windows onto the playground. The CD player sang Mozart. Mrs. Cotton put her elbows on her desk and held her hands in front of her, fingertips to fingertips, as if she were praying. Abi wondered if she was ill.

She looked at her classmates. Many of them seemed to be throwing questioning looks around, but Mrs. Cotton was quiet, and there were no answers. Abi drew a picture of her Grandma's house in Parkerton, making little green circles for her rock-lawn.

Mrs. Cotton tried again. "Maybe we'll play a game," she said.

Abi put her colored pencils down and waited for the game to be announced.

"Maybe not," Mrs. Cotton said.

Abi went back to her picture, drawing Grandma's RV parked in front of her mobile home, with the big mountain looming in the background like a giant ready to pounce.

Orchestra was canceled that day.

That night at dinner, Mom served spaghetti with meatballs, garlic bread, and salad. She had a veggie burger and a bowl of fresh spinach.

"One hundred fifty-nine," Mom said.

"Good job," said Dad, proud of her.

"Mrs. Cotton didn't talk to us all afternoon," Abi said. "I think she is sick."

"Oh, no," Dad said. "Sick teachers are not what I need. It is very hard these days to get substitutes."

Will sucked long spaghetti strands into his mouth. "Dad," he said, "why is it your job to get subs this year? You haven't had to do it in other years. Isn't it the principal's job?"

"Usually," Dad said, "but this year is different. Mrs. Robbins had to take over some of the high school English courses, so she's busier than she used to be."

"It can be hard in a small school," Mom said. "We all pitch in when we can. Dad gets the subs, and that eases Mrs. Robbins's load. Abi makes Dad's lunches, and that eases Dad's load. And so on."

"In what way did Mrs. Cotton seem ill, Punkin?" Dad asked, getting back to the subject.

"She was late getting back from lunch for one thing. Then she didn't talk to us all afternoon. She tried to read to us, but then she stopped. She let us draw and read until the end of the day. And then we didn't have orchestra."

"Hmm," Dad said. "Doesn't sound good, but it might not be sickness. She might have had bad news. Or maybe her cat was going to have kittens at any minute and she was worried. Or maybe the Internal Revenue Service is on her case."

"I know, maybe her house burned down during lunch and she was preoccupied about it," Will said, and Abi laughed.

"Maybe she left her headlights on all day and her battery was dead and she was afraid of telling Mr. Cotton," Abi said.

Dad cleared his throat. "I know," he said. "She found out that she had gained three pounds. That would put Mom into distraction."

"Mark!" Mom said, but Abi came to Mrs. Cotton's defense. "She did not gain three pounds," Abi said. "She never gains weight. She is thin and beautiful."

"Chubby can be beautiful," Mom said.

"Absolutely," Dad said.

"What is that supposed to mean?" Mom said, stabbing her spinach leaf.

And so on. Abi smiled and let it happen around her, calm now that she realized there was probably nothing seriously wrong with Mrs. Cotton. Probably nothing that a good night's sleep wouldn't cure.

They had just sat down in the living room for family devotions when the telephone rang.

"Hello," Mom said. "Oh, hi, Iris."

Abi stiffened and looked over at Dad. He was already on his feet to take the call. Mrs. Cotton must be ill after all. But Mom didn't ask Dad to take the phone.

"Really?" she said. "Just a minute, Iris; I want to change phones."

Mom told Dad to hang up the phone after she'd picked up the phone in the bedroom. Then, they all sat there waiting for Mom to come back.

"Guess we'll get a sub tomorrow," Abi said.

"Guess so," said Dad.

Mom didn't come out for a long time. When she did, her eyes were red. She sat back down in her chair and opened her Bible. As Dad read, Abi looked over at Mom, wondering what had made Mom cry. Mom kept her eyes down and gave no hint.

After prayer time, Mom got up and sang herself into the kitchen. She pulled out all the makings of chocolate chip cookies. Abi cracked the eggs and poured in the chocolate chips.

"Just tell me one thing, Ellen," Dad said, reaching his finger out to hook a blob of batter. "Do I need to find a sub?"

"No sub," said Mom, smiling. "I'll tell you later."

That night, many thoughts crowded into Abi's mind. She worried about Mrs. Cotton. Mom hadn't said anything more about her telephone conversation with Mrs. Cotton. And when Mom cuddled in with her for a few minutes at bedtime, she'd had something else to talk about.

"I've talked with Dad about Grandma's idea for you to visit her over Christmas vacation." Mom took a deep breath. "We've decided that you may not miss Christmas with our family."

"Oh." Abi's voice was small and hurt.

"But," Mom said, "if we can convince Grandma to stay here until December twenty-sixth, then you can go home with her in her RV and fly back later."

"But that will only give me a few days at Grandma's."

"Dad says maybe you can stay two weeks at Grandma's. It will mean you'll get back a few days late for the beginning of school, but Dad and I think it would be worth it for you to have the experience."

Abi grinned. "Thanks."

"Dad also says you have to earn one quarter of your airfare. Grandma said she'd pay half. That leaves one quarter for Dad to pay and another quarter for you to earn."

Abi sat up straight in bed. "How much will it be?"

"I've called around. It looks like the lowest airfare is about two hundred dollars for a one-way flight, so you'll need to earn fifty dollars."

"How will I . . . "

"You can do it," Mom said. "Remember about working to a high standard?"

"Yes, but fifty dollars? I only have ten dollars in my bank right now. That leaves forty dollars!"

"You think about it. If I know you, you'll find a way."

Mom kissed her and said good night. Abi lay on her pillow, clutching her stuffed bear and thinking hard. She usually made money by doing "quarter jobs" around the house. Forty dollars would be one hundred and sixty quarter jobs. Was there time?

She thought about how she could earn the money and how scared she would be to fly home by herself on a big airplane. As she got sleepier, other thoughts drifted through her mind. She thought about Tamika's party the following night.

She thought about what a slug Jerry Walters was. She thought about the announcement that had been made in orchestra a few days ago.

"I'd like to do something special at our Christmas concert," Mrs. Cotton had said. "Listen. Normally, the orchestra plays, and other than the short solo section by the concertmaster or concertmistress—" here she had nodded to Tamika—"there have not been any individual performances. I'd like to change that this year."

She remembered her heart beating hard when Mrs. Cotton had said this.

"I've been thinking this through," Mrs. Cotton continued, "and I believe I'd like to have a special group piece, such as a trio or duet, and then, one honor soloist. I want someone who can really turn on the music, a real big flourishing piece. Classical or Christmas. Maybe something you've studied in your private lessons. Be thinking about this. We'll audition in a few weeks."

Abi had certainly been thinking about this. If she could be the honor soloist for the Christmas program, that would make up for not being concertmistress. It would be better than being concertmistress. The more she lay on her bed and thought, the more Abi determined she would get the honor solo. *I'll meet Mrs. Cotton's high standards,* she thought. *I can do it.*

After she had thought about these things for a while, she noticed that she was thirsty. She got up and walked barefoot to her bedroom door, opened it quietly, and slipped across the hall to the bathroom. But before she could turn on the water, she heard voices from the kitchen. Mom and Dad were talking.

"Isn't it wonderful," Mom said. "And after seven years!"

"It's good," Dad said. "It's wonderful. It's terrific. But I just can't help thinking how difficult it's going to be for Abi to have another teacher this year. And, how hard it's going to be for me to find another substitute, especially for such a long time. Last I heard from Brad Doyle, he's going to be gone all year."

"Well, don't worry about it, Mark," said Mom. "It's not until April. And you can cross that bridge when you get there."

"True," said Dad. "And God will provide."

"He always does."

Abi's heart jumped in her chest, like a jack-in-the-box let loose. She understood what Mom and Dad were saying. She forgot about her thirst, crept back into her bedroom, and sunk back down into her pillows. She tried to be happy for Mrs. Cotton.

When Mrs. Cotton told the class her news—a full week later—Abi pretended to be surprised. She tried to be happy. But mostly, she was sorry that Mrs. Cotton would be leaving school in early spring.

"I'm going to be having a baby sometime in April," she said. Her smile lit the room like sunshine.

Abi felt Mrs. Cotton's happiness floating over her, trying to settle down on her. Mrs. Cotton reminded the class that this was only October, that there would be many months ahead of her, and that she would be with them until April.

"But I may get a bit waddly and, uh, fat, so be kind to me, okay?"

Some of the kids laughed, but Abi sat silently, willing herself to remember this was only October. She would have her wonderful teacher for several more months. And then, there would just be a few weeks until school got out.

"What will you name it?" Mindy asked. Abi shot her a glance of horror. Mom always said not to ask adults personal questions. Like how old they are, or how much they weigh, or what they are planning to name their baby. However, Mrs. Cotton didn't seem to mind.

"I don't know," she said. "Right now we're just calling it our April baby."

9 Tamika's Party

"Okay, okay," Louby said, "everyone sit down. We are going to see if this white girl can play the violin."

Everyone hooted, and Abi smiled. "Do it, Abi," Tamika said. "Give them your Bach."

So Abi played her Bach A Minor Concerto, first movement, the best she'd ever played it without the CD playing along.

"Whoa, the girl can play," Louby said.

"See," said Tamika. "I told you. She's the best violinist in my school."

Abi turned to Tamika; her mouth dropped open wide at this praise.

She thinks I'm the best.

"Enough music," Mrs. Mitchell said, entering the room with a gigantic bowl of popcorn. "It's time to see who has the biggest mouth. James, come in here in case someone chokes."

Abi was glad to have a medical doctor handy for this type of experiment.

"Everyone at the same time. Now, one," Mrs. Mitchell counted, and each girl took a piece of popcorn and put it in her mouth. "Two . . . three . . . four," and so on. "Fifteen, sixteen."

At seventeen, Marla choked and spat all her popcorn out on the floor. This made Louby laugh, but she kept her popcorn in her mouth. At eighteen Abi stopped, but didn't know what to do. She couldn't chew it, couldn't speak to ask for help, and definitely did not want to spit popcorn.

Marla nudged her with her elbow. "Just spit it out, sister. Otherwise you'll die of suffocation."

She blushed, and spat the popcorn onto her jeans.

"Twenty-two, twenty-three."

Jackie was the winner at twenty-five pieces of popcorn. Everyone clapped.

Dr. Mitchell grabbed a broom and swept the popcorn from the hardwood floor.

"I've got the best idea ever," Louby said. "We're going to braid Abi's hair. Beads and all!"

Abi shrank back against the wall, but all the other girls agreed. Thirty minutes later she felt tugged and pulled to pieces, since all the girls had been braiding her hair at once.

"Gorgeous," Marla said. "Take a look."

Abi laughed when she saw herself in the mirror. She shook her hair from side to side and liked how it felt to have the beaded braids flying around her.

"Ahem," Dr. Mitchell said. He walked around Abi, a grin on his face. "You're not taking this hairstyle up as a fashion statement, are you?"

Abi laughed. "No, sir."

"Good," he said. He sat down at the piano. "Let's have some music, girls. We'll start with 'The Farmer in the Dell.' "

"Is it opera time, Papa?" Tamika asked, eyes shining.

"Of course," Dr. Mitchell replied.

"Get the pillows," Louby called.

So they sang "The Farmer in the Dell" in wild, operatic voices, pillows under their shirts because, so said Louby, most women who sing opera are fat. After a minute's hesitation, Abi joined in the abandoned singing, pushing her voice to a wide vibrato.

"Ooh, Abi, you are one good singer," Marla said.

When Mrs. Mitchell came into the room with her camera, the girls stuck their pillowed stomachs out and flung their arms wide as if singing a finale.

"The Cheese stands alone, the Cheese stands alone . . . " the piano music slowed, and the girls took the cue. They planted their feet and belted out the last line:

"Heigh-ho the dairy-o, the Cheese stands alone!"

Then they all collapsed into a giggling pile. Abi laughed so hard, she was afraid she wouldn't be able to breathe.

Dinner was next, pizza delivered. Abi ate four pieces of extra-cheese-pepperoni-pineapple. She downed two tall glasses of soda pop.

"Hey," said Jackie, "let's tell the scariest thing that's ever happened to us. I'll start. When I was six years old, we moved to a brand-new neighborhood. All the houses looked alike, so the first time I walked home from school, I didn't know which house was mine!"

"Oh, very scary," Marla said. "What happened?"

"I went down the side of the street I knew our house was on, and I knocked on every door. When the door opened and it wasn't my mom, I ran away. When I finally got to the right house and my mom answered the door, I burst into tears. But my mom said, 'Why did you knock, honey? This is your house; just come on in!' "

A loud laugh split the air. "That is hilarious," said Louby. "That is the funniest thing I ever heard."

"I think it's terrible," said Tamika. "But it's not the worst thing." She looked around the circle of girls. "Listen to this. When I was eight years old, I went on a spinning ride at the fair. The ride got stuck when I was at the top of the circle, way, way up above the ground. They couldn't get the ride going for a while. My hands started slipping. I felt like I was going to fall to the ground and die. What about you, Abi?"

Abi thought back to that time when she was horribly scared. She didn't know if she should bring it up at a party.

"When I was seven years old, my grandpa died," she said. "It was at a Fourth of July picnic. He was playing his bassoon in a band, and he had a heart attack or something. He shouted, fell down, and was dead."

"And you saw this?"

"Everyone saw it," she said. "It was terrible."

"Oh," the girls said. "Sorry."

"My grandpa died a long time ago," Tamika said. "I never knew him. I wish he had lived because then maybe he and Grandma Sunshine would come to see us here. Mom says they used to travel when Grandpa was alive."

"Yes, they did," Mrs. Mitchell said. "They went everywhere. But now, you know, Grandma Sunshine won't travel out of Missouri."

"Why not?" Louby said. "Is she afraid? And why is she called Grandma Sunshine?"

"She is afraid, actually," said Mrs. Mitchell. "And she's called Grandma Sunshine because it's her name. Sunshine Mitchell."

Abi smiled and wished her grandma had a name like Sunshine instead of Vada.

"But I wish she would come here," Tamika said. "Like for the Christmas concert. She's never heard me play my violin."

"That's sad," Abi said. How sad, she thought. Grandma Johnson had heard her play many times. Sometimes she flew to Fairlawn. Other times she drove her RV. And when the Crims visited her in Parkerton, Grandma would borrow instruments from her friends so she could hear Will and Abi play.

"In Parkerton," she would say, "you can find a violin or cello or anything else you want. Everyone is so old, they've collected everything there is!"

"One time I asked her to come," Tamika said. "But maybe I didn't say it right, because if she knew how much I wanted her to come, like for Christmas this year, when I have that little solo, I bet she would come."

"Never mind, Tamika," Dr. Mitchell said gently. "We can send her a videotape so she can watch you."

"It's not the same."

"Speaking of scariest moments," Dr. Mitchell said, changing the subject, "when I was a kid, I had five brothers and . . . "

Just then the phone rang. It was for Abi.

"Take it in the back hall, Abi," Mrs. Mitchell said, so Abi walked down the long hall to the telephone, with Dr. Mitchell's scary story about his brothers fading out.

"Hello," she said.

It was Mom, wondering how everything was going. She answered her questions in one-syllable words: "yes," "fine," not paying attention. Her eyes had fallen on a list taped to the telephone table. The list was titled Important Family Numbers. One name on the list gave her an idea—a wonderful idea! As soon as Mom said "good-bye, honey," Abi tore a sheet of paper from the memo pad. Quickly, she scribbled down Grandma Sunshine's address and phone number. She turned quickly into Tamika's room, tucked the paper inside her violin case, closed it as quietly as she could, and then rejoined the party.

Everyone was laughing.

"So you can bet they never did that again!" Dr. Mitchell said. "That's what they get for picking on the littlest brother."

She didn't ask what the scary moment had been.

"Everything okay, Abi?" Mrs. Mitchell said.

"Yes, ma'am."

Tamika jumped up. "Mom," she said, "it's nine o'clock." Her eyes were shining.

"Right, girl. Tradition time!"

All the girls jumped up and ran outside. Abi followed, not knowing why. The swimming pool lay before them, quiet and still. A few scattered leaves floated on the top.

"One, two . . ." Mrs. Mitchell said.

"Wait," Abi said. "What's happening?"

"Oh that's right; you haven't been here before," Tamika said. "At every party, we all jump in the pool with all our clothes on at nine o'clock."

"One, two," Mrs. Mitchell said, "three!"

Five girls jumped in. Abi jumped up and grabbed her knees in front of her to do a cannonball. As she splashed down into the water, she realized how happy she was that she'd come. It had been a wonderful party.

"It was neat to be at a party where we did a lot of things and didn't just sit around talking," she told Mom.

"Good thing to keep in mind," Mom said, "for the next time you have a party."

Abi smiled. When her birthday arrived in March, she would invite all the girls in her class—even Mindy—and all the girls she'd met tonight. They'd play wonderful games and play opera.

"We don't have a pool, though," she said.

"So you can pour water on your heads," said Mom. "But never mind. It's bedtime, and your birthday is months away. Now, take those beads out of your hair, okay?"

Abi strung all the beads from her hair onto a string. Then she reached under her bed for her box of special things. "Thank you, Tamika," she said, as she carefully placed the string of beads in her treasure box.

Late that night, when the whole house was quiet and everyone was asleep, Abi awoke. She opened her violin case cautiously, so the latches didn't make much noise, and pulled out the folded sheet of paper. She sat down at her desk, turned on her desk light, and smoothed out the paper. Then, she pulled a piece of writing paper from her desk and wrote:

Dear Mrs. Sunshine Mitchell,

Your granddaughter, Tamika, is my wonderful friend. She wishes you would come for our Christmas concert. Maybe it is scary for you to fly, but Tamika went backstage to get Pinchas Zukerman's autograph. Maybe she got her courage from you. Please try to come. Did you know that Tamika is the concertmistress of our orchestra? She will play a solo, "Thou Didst Leave Thy Throne." She says you have never heard her play. I hope you can come.

Sincerely,

Abi Crim

In the morning, she rode her bike to the post office. She bought a stamp from the stamp machine, stuck it to the envelope, and dropped the letter into the slot marked Out of Town Mail.

"There," she said aloud. "We'll see what happens now."

10 Mrs. Mom

When Abi didn't hear anything from Grandma Sunshine, she felt foolish and tried to put the letter out of her mind. What had she been thinking of anyway, to write a letter like that to someone she had never met? What if Grandma Sunshine told Dr. Mitchell about her letter? He was a doctor. He would figure out that she had copied the address from their family list and perhaps be angry. Maybe he wouldn't let Tamika invite her over any more. She didn't mention the letter to anyone, not even Kimberly.

And so, in the slow way of fall, the weeks went on. Abi went to school happy, worked hard, practiced hard, and talked over her days with Kimberly. They wore sweaters now when they sat out on the porch and talked about Abi's Bach concerto and her quarter jobs and Kimberly's leaf collection.

"I'm trying to get leaves of every color. Red, green, purple, orange, yellow. I got a brown one too, but it's crunchy."

Abi laughed. "I wish I could do a leaf collection. We have to catch fifty bugs next semester. Maybe I'll stay with Grandma and never come back. That'll save me having to hunt around for creepy crawly things."

"Nope," Kimberly said laughing. "You are not allowed to stay at your grandma's house very long. My life is too quiet without you. Me and Mom alone in the big house. You can't

. imagine. It's quiet all the time. When I do my schoolwork, it's quiet. When I don't do my schoolwork, it's quiet. I need you for the noise."

"Oh," Abi said. "I'm the noise in your life. Great."

"Yeah, sort of." Then the girls looked at each other and laughed.

"We're almost like sisters, but we don't fight," Kimberly said. It grew quiet at the word *sister*. It was a subject they had never discussed, until now.

"I found out I had a sister once," Abi said. "Her name was Marigold."

"I had a sister once too."

Abi remembered. She and Kimberly never talked about those days three years ago. She had shadowy memories of the awful week when Mrs. Edison had been crying and Kimberly was crying, and Mr. Edison and little Marie never got home from the store. The black dresses, the cars, the flowers.

She reached over and hugged Kimberly. "I'm sorry."

"Me too."

October faded into November. Abi racked up quarter jobs, practiced her concerto whenever she could, and spent lots of time with Kimberly, just talking. Since their talk about sisters, they had talked about other things, like boys, like parents, like friends. Like Mrs. Cotton.

Mrs. Cotton stopped wearing tailored suits and left her belts at home. She did, however, keep wearing bold, happy colors, and bright African prints. Abi was glad that expecting a baby had not made Mrs. Cotton slow down or stop being wonderful.

Mrs. Cotton stopped tacking Abi's spelling-sentence papers on the *Good Work!* board after the first three.

"It looks bad," she said, "if I put the same person's paper on the board every week."

"That's okay," Abi told her. "I don't need to be on the board."

Just knowing her papers were meeting Mrs. Cotton's expectations made her happy.

Her airfare quarters began to pile up. She had settled into working steadily on quarter jobs—picking weeds, washing windows, vacuuming the house—one at a time, to earn her part of the money for the airfare back home from Grandma's house. She made a chart on the computer spreadsheet program listing the numbers one through one hundred sixty. Next to each number she listed the job she did and the date. Then there was a space for Mom's initials to indicate that the job had been done up to Mom's expectations. By the middle of November, she had done almost one hundred quarter jobs, and there were still several weeks to go.

There were exceptions to her happy sixth-grade life during these fall weeks. Mindy refused to play four-square with her at recess. Jerry continued to make fun of her spelling papers, her insistence on studying her Bach concerto whenever there was free reading time, her eating lunch with Tamika.

Abi viewed Jerry as a slug mired in deep slugness. Or Slugity. She hadn't decided what Jerry's condition should be called. Sluggery? No, that would be a place where slugs were kept.

Jerry the Slug. He was always oozing around the sixth grade, leaving a trail of verbal slime. The chapel speaker told her to try to love the unlovable people she knew, but no matter how hard she tried, she could not work up a love for Jerry Walters. She couldn't even work up a like for him.

"Well," Mom said, when Abi asked her about it, "there are different ways to show God's love for people. Try being kind. You don't know his whole situation. Be nice." Abi agreed to try.

All together, things were going very well. She was striving for excellence in her music and her schoolwork. She was working hard to be a good friend at school and a sister-friend to Kimberly at home.

It's turning out to be the year of me after all.

Daylight-saving time ended, so she woke up in the dark. The days grew cooler and the nights longer. Mom rummaged around in the attic for the boxes marked *Winter Clothes.*

"It's not winter yet," she said, "but it's best to be prepared. This time of year, a cold day can snap out at you from nowhere, and you don't want to be digging through junk in the attic when it's freezing outside."

Such a day came in mid-November, when most of the leaves had fallen off the trees. The Crims' lawn was carpeted in an orange-red-purple-yellow softness, and there were great big blue-sky gaps in the trees.

Mrs. Cotton seemed unusually thoughtful that day. She would stop sometimes in the middle of a sentence for a few seconds, then smile her wonderful smile and continue to teach. The day melted into past participles, exponential numbers, early Chinese history, and the periodic table of elements.

After school, Abi plopped into her seat in the second violins and smiled at Tamika in her concertmistress's chair.

Tamika had new beads in her hair today—orange and brown and yellow—"for fall," she said. "I'm trying to be seasonal."

Mrs. Cotton mounted the conductor's step with what Abi thought was a bit of hesitance. But maybe not.

"Hi," she said. "How are my happy musicians today?"

"Happy," they all said.

Somehow, this had become the usual orchestra beginning. Everyone laughed, just like every day. Mrs. Cotton prayed that God would give them a successful and enjoyable rehearsal.

"Before we begin," she said, "I have a few announcements. First, my other orchestra—the one at the Phipps Center—will also be having a Christmas concert. It will be during the first week of Christmas vacation. I'm telling you now so you can make plans to come if you're not going away for vacation. I think you'll enjoy the concert. It will be different music from what we play here, of course.

"I'll get some flyers to you as soon as I get them back from the printer. How many of you will be in town during vacation?"

Many hands went up around the orchestra. Abi raised her hand.

"Okay, that's good. Now, how many of you are working on pieces to audition for the duet and solo at our Christmas program?"

Hands went up from every section.

"That's wonderful. I know you'll all do wonderfully at the audition, and I am looking forward to hearing you play." She tapped her music stand with her conductor's baton. "And now, why don't we play some music before our time is up?"

Mrs. Cotton breathed deeply. She bent a little from side to side, hardly noticeably. She rubbed her hand across her forehead, and then placed it on her belly. A strange, vacant look came into her eyes. Then, she fixed the orchestra with a thoughtful look and brought up her hands for the "instruments up" signal. Abi tucked her violin under her chin and waited for the downbeat, her third finger pressed onto her D string, her eyes locked on Mrs. Cotton's face. Was she dreaming, or did Mrs. Cotton's face seem faraway and almost sad?

"Do this for me, kids," Mrs. Cotton said. "Pretend it's our last practice together, that we'll never see each other again, and we want to play magnificently for each other."

Abi wondered if Mrs. Cotton were ill. Was she going to go home this evening and die? But Abi bent her head to the music and played as Mrs. Cotton had asked, with every bit of music she had inside of her. Everyone else must have felt the same way. The sound that soared and dipped around them was true, clear, and perfect.

"Thanks, people," Mrs. Cotton said, smiling a gentle smile. "That was truly wonderful."

Abi walked home from orchestra practice slowly, kicking a rock in front of her, wondering what was wrong with Mrs. Cotton. Something certainly was wrong. Teachers didn't get up and say "pretend this is the last time we'll see each other" unless something was terribly wrong. Maybe Mr. Cotton got transferred to another city and they would be moving. One of Abi's friends had moved away in third grade when her father was transferred to Florida. Or maybe Mr. Cotton thought his wife was overdoing things. Maybe he'd told her she had to make a choice between working at the Phipps Center and working at Fairlawn Christian School. Mrs. Cotton would choose Phipps, of course, because she'd been there longer, and that was how she became Channel 7's Person of the Week.

At dinner Abi didn't know whether she should tell Dad that Mrs. Cotton was never coming back. No, if that were true, Mrs. Cotton would call him and tell him soon enough. Then Dad would have to hurry up and find another substitute for tomorrow, for ever.

Please, Dad, anyone but Mrs. Baumble.

She swirled juice around in her glass and tried to focus her mind on what homework she had this evening and whether she would have time to get any quarter jobs done.

When Mom suddenly said, "one hundred fifty-three," Abi shook her head.

"No," Abi said. "Only one hundred thirteen."

"One thirteen? Never in a million years," Mom said. "I'll be glad with one forty-nine, believe you me."

Abi felt her face grow hot, realizing that Mom was thinking about weight, not quarter jobs. Not her trip to Grandma's and how Abi was going to pay for it.

"That's great, both of you," Dad said. "Pounds and quarter jobs all around."

"Good job, Mom," Will said. "You're almost there. Pretty soon we won't be able to find you." He got up from the table and pretended to stumble around the kitchen saying, "Where's Mom? I can't find Mom! She's dieted herself to extinction."

"Sit down, William," Mom said, but she was laughing.

Abi wondered what would happen when Mom got to one forty-nine. Would Abi recognize her? Would she wear all new clothes? Would she be a happier, more beautiful Mom? To Abi, Mom looked the same as she looked a few weeks ago when she said, "One sixty-two." Same old comfortable Mom. Abi took a bit of teriyaki chicken and calculated how long it would take her to complete the remaining forty-seven jobs.

"Your efforts are really paying off," Dad said.

Abi said, "Thanks," at the same time Mom did, and everyone laughed. Abi felt hot again, and felt small and silly for thinking Dad had been talking to her, wishing dinner were over so she could wonder about Mrs. Cotton in peace, deciding not to say anything more at dinner.

"How much longer?" Dad said. Abi tried to concentrate on her rice and not look around. She didn't want to embarrass herself three times during one meal.

"Abi," Dad said, "how much time do you have to finish the jobs?"

"Not long," Abi said. "But I'll work harder."

Dad smiled. "You'll make it."

"Me, too," said Mom. "Abi and I will both reach our goals before Grandma comes." And she smiled her best Mom-smile at Abi, the one that made Abi feel proud and happy. Abi smiled back.

Then the phone rang.

"Every time we sit down to dinner, that phone . . ." Dad began.

"Hello," Mom said.

"Oh," she said.

"Oh no." Her voice shook.

Then, as Abi watched her, she saw, quite distinctly, Mom's back straighten. And she heard, quite distinctly, Mom's voice change from one of surprise and sadness to one of steely resolve.

"Iris," she said, and Abi jumped when she heard it, "I will be right there. Don't you move and don't you worry. We will do whatever needs to be done."

"Mark," she said, turning to her dad who was staring at her, mesmerized, it seemed, by the iron in her voice. "I am going to see Iris. I may . . ." she paused a long while and nodded her head as if talking to herself and answering, "be gone for several hours. I will tell you everything when I return. Right now, there's not time."

"Just tell me this," Dad said weakly. He took a deep breath. "Do I need to try to find a substitute for Mrs. Cotton?"

Mom paused for the briefest instant. "No," she said firmly. "No, you do not."

"Good," Dad said. "At the moment, I'm plumb out of subs."

Mom stared at Dad in a way Abi could not interpret, then grabbed her purse and ran outside, the door slamming behind her.

Dad, Will, and Abi looked at each other with shrugs and hand motions that meant, "What in the world?"

Dad said, "Mom has something on her mind and up her sleeve, but don't worry. All will be well. I've seen her in this mode before. It doesn't happen often, but when it does, believe me, something big is about to change in the family."

"I remember last time," Will said. He flung himself full-length on the couch. "Remember, Dad? Mom got very excited and quiet and ran out of the house when I was ten. I remember it clearly."

"Don't remind me!"

"Yes, she did, and when she came back, her hair was red!"

"No," Abi said.

"It's true," Dad said. "But I have a feeling she's not coloring her hair tonight."

"I have that feeling too," Will said. "But something tells me whatever she's doing, it's big."

I have that feeling too.

Abi finished drinking her glass of milk, then silently washed the dinner dishes and did her homework. Then she e-mailed Grandma.

Dear Grandma, (she wrote)

Mom has gone out for the evening, but I don't know why. She wouldn't tell! I think maybe Mrs. Cotton (my teacher) is sick. She is also pregnant. She is wonderful. I love her. She is the best teacher in the world, and she wears bee-oo-tiful clothes. I would like to be like her when I grow up, except I am white.

I have decided to do three quarter jobs a day, which is seventy-five cents a day. I have decided to practice hard so I can play the solo in the Christmas concert.

Love, Abi

P.S. See you soon.

Before Abi sent the e-mail, she erased the sentence about the Christmas concert. She wanted her solo to be a surprise for Grandma.

Abi was still up, doing a final check of her math homework, when Mom came home at ten o'clock. Abi screamed when she saw her. Dad gasped. Will said, "Mom!"

Mom's hair was not red. It was still brown, but it was cut very short, and she carried four large shopping bags from the mall.

"Don't just stand there, Abi," Mom said. "Help me put away these new clothes."

"Ellen," Dad's voice was low, but firm, "knowing you as I do, I assume that there is a very good explanation for your cutting all your beautiful hair off and spending half a paycheck on clothes. Why in the world have you done this?"

"Now, Mark," she said, turning to him with that same steel-backbone resolve Abi had seen earlier this evening, "you don't expect me to teach sixth grade for the rest of the school year fussing with long hair and with no decent professional working clothes, do you?"

Dad sat back suddenly in his chair. Then, quietly, "Well, no, Ellen. I wouldn't expect that."

But Abi had barely heard him. The strength had drained out of her body when Mom had said those astounding words, "teach sixth grade for the rest of the school year." Abi's nose tingled. Her throat felt like it was getting smaller and smaller. She swallowed hard, bit her lip, and stared at Dad, pleading WHY.

"What's wrong with Mrs. Cotton, Mom?" Will said.

"The babies are in danger, Will. Iris's doctor has ordered her to stay absolutely flat in bed until April," Mom's voice was fierce, protective, "if the babies hold on that long."

"Babies?" Abi whispered.

"Three," Mom said, holding up three fingers. And then tears spilled out of Mom's eyes onto her cheeks, and she looked Dad straight in the eyes.

"We are going to do what we can to save Iris's triplets, Mark."

Dad and Mom locked eyes without speaking. Dad nodded.

Abi knew the word that passed silently between them: *Marigold.*

"Well, then," Dad said, clearing his throat, "we need to get an early start in the morning. Let's ask God to help us, and let's get ourselves to bed."

In the morning Will and Abi didn't walk to school. They got into the car with Mom, drove to school, and parked in the teachers' parking lot. Mom and Abi walked to the sixth-grade classroom. Abi stumbled to her seat.

"What's going on, Abi?" Several students asked her. "Where's Mrs. Cotton?"

Abi hardly heard Mom as she called the roll. As she prayed. As she explained what was happening. As she gave the assignments. The day rolled by in a fog.

Abi made dinner while Mom called Mrs. Cotton.

"It was just fine, Iris," she said. "Don't worry one thing about it. What did I get a teaching degree for if not for this very moment? Why did I take a conducting class in college if not for this instant?"

Then, "Yes, that's a great idea. Perfect. I'll tell them to-morrow."

"Tell us what?" Abi asked, after Mom had hung up the telephone.

"I'll tell you tomorrow," she said. "At home, I'm just Mom."

"One hundred fifty-one," Mom announced at dinner.

Abi bit her lip. She had done one hundred seventeen quarter jobs, but she didn't say anything.

11 Audition

"All right," Mom said. "Does everyone understand how the auditions will work?"

Heads nodded. Abi nodded. Mom had just explained Mrs. Cotton's idea.

The auditions would be tape-recorded, and the tapes numbered and sent to Mrs. Cotton to judge. Mrs. Cotton would not know who was playing on each tape. She would send her list of the winners back when she'd chosen them. It sounded simple and fair.

After that, kids spent every spare minute practicing. Some practiced during recess. Duets practiced during lunch break, leaving sandwiches barely touched. Soloists rushed to the auditorium after school to get in a few precious moments of practice before rehearsal began.

"I'm ready," Abi told Kimberly the night before auditions. "I know this concerto backward and forward. I hear it in my sleep. I dream about the notes on the page."

"You'll be wonderful," Kimberly said. "I can't wait to see your grandma's face when she watches you play it at the concert."

Abi smiled. "She will be proud of me."

"I'll be proud of you too."

And then it was Wednesday, the day before Thanksgiving. Audition day.

All the students who were not in orchestra had gone home, had already started their four-day weekend. Orchestra students who were not trying out for the honor solo and duet were not required to attend the audition, so the auditorium was not as full as usual. The room seemed larger that way. Kids sat apart from one another, looking at their music for one last time, picking their violins and violas guitar-like. Cellists leaned their heads close to their fingerboards and plucked quietly. One bassist sat on a stool plucking strings and looking off into the emptiness of the room.

Abi tuned her violin carefully at the piano, one string at a time. She felt shaky.

Another audition to be won or lost. This is my chance to make Mrs. Cotton proud of me. To meet a higher standard.

Mom set up a microphone. There would be no music stand, as all music had to be memorized. Mrs. Fowler sat at the piano, ready to play as needed. Some mothers were there also, the ones who would be accompanying their children.

"I will give each of you a number," Mom said, handing out slips of numbered papers. "The number you get will be the order in which you play today. Also, that same number will be written on the tape that will be sent to Mrs. Cotton for adjudication. Mrs. Cotton will not know who is playing when she judges the entries. Is everyone clear on this?"

Everyone was clear. At last all the numbers were passed out. Abi was number eight. The auditions began.

Mindy and Amy played a duet with Amy's mother accompanying. It was very good.

Two fifth-grade girls played "Jingle Bells." It was an interesting arrangement, with lots of pizzicato and a great double-stop at the end. Mrs. Fowler played the piano for them. Then, three other duets played, all of them accompanied by Mrs. Fowler.

When Mom called "six," Tamika rose. She walked to the front of the stage. She did not hand any music to Mrs. Fowler to play. She nodded at Mom to start the tape, then tucked her violin under her chin, put bow to string, and began.

Abi closed her eyes as Tamika's music flowed over her, clear and perfect. Tamika played "Jesu, Joy of Man's Desiring," a slow piece by Bach that Abi had always loved.

Every Christmas of her life, Abi could remember Dad playing a recording of this piece, could remember sitting on the couch swaying to the slow perfection of it. When Tamika finished, Abi sighed. She didn't hear number seven play.

"Eight," Mom said.

Abi stood. She smiled at Tamika. Mrs. Fowler took Mom's place at the tape recorder so Mom could play the piano. Abi took her place in the center of the stage, fit her instrument under her chin, closed her eyes for just a moment, then nodded at Mom and began.

She played fiercely, as if her whole life had pointed to this moment. As if everything depended on this one performance. As if she were auditioning for the New York Philharmonic.

She placed each finger perfectly, played the eighth and sixteenth notes without mistake, moved flawlessly from first to third positions. Her vibrato was rich and true, her bowings long and effortless. It was a moment of triumph. When she finished, she knew she had played better than she had ever played before. If she had been a boy, she would have punched the sky with happiness and whooped her joy out loud.

That evening Grandma Johnson drove up the Crims' driveway in her motor home. Abi ran out to greet her. She tried and failed to keep her joy inside.

"Grandma, I think I won the audition for honor solo!"

"If you did, I'll be the proudest grandma in the whole world." She kissed Abi's head. "Grandpa would have been proud of you too. I wish he could have heard you play."

The next day, Thanksgiving, Mom announced that she weighed one hundred and forty-eight pounds, and Abi mentioned that when she mopped the floor that night, she would have completed all one hundred sixty quarter jobs. She was filled to overflowing with happiness. Grandma was here. Abi would be going home with her after Christmas. Two weeks alone with Grandma—she could hardly bear the excitement of it. And between now and then—the concert. My concert, she thought.

As usual, they all ate too much at Thanksgiving dinner. They talked about everything, from Will's latest talk with the Air Force recruiter to Grandma's reports on the shuffleboard teams in Parkerton. They stayed up very late playing Monopoly, Battleship, and endless games of Rook.

Abi worked hard to keep her mind on the holiday, to enjoy her days off with her family, but as the days of the Thanksgiving weekend passed, her mind was filled more and more with the Bach A Minor Concerto for solo violin and how she would play it at the Christmas concert.

On the Tuesday after Thanksgiving, Mom announced the results in orchestra rehearsal.

"I have a letter here from Mrs. Cotton," Mom said. Kids sat up in their seats. Some looked around. Abi bit her lip and tried to pretend her insides were not eaten up with nervousness.

"In the duet category, the winner was group number three, and the runner-up group was number one. Who was group number three, please?"

Two fifth-grade girls—a violist and a cellist—stood.

"Ah, good work. Congratulations to Chloe and Elaine. And who was in the runner-up group, number one?"

Mindy and Amy raised their hands.

"Good work, girls," Mom said. "Keep practicing together. Runners-up play if the first-place winner gets sick or has an emergency and can't play."

Mindy and Amy looked at each other and smiled a smile that seemed to say, "Oh well, maybe next time."

"Now, let's see. The honor soloist." Mom pretended to fumble with the letter, turning it upside down as if it were written in code.

"Come on, Mrs. Crim," someone said; "you're killing us."

"Ah," Mom said, smiling. "The runner-up for honor soloist is number six. Who is number six?"

Tamika raised her hand and was applauded by the orchestra.

"Keep practicing that beautiful piece, Tamika, in case the honor soloist is unable to play on concert night."

Tamika smiled and looked over at Abi. Abi grinned back, her heart filled with happiness. If Tamika hadn't won, she knew she must have.

At last I've done it. It's the year of Abi Crim after all.

"And, the honor soloist for the Christmas concert this year will be number eight. Number eight, please stand."

Abi stood, trembling with joy, while the applause of her friends—and her mother—surrounded her.

There was china on the dinner table that night.

12 The Concert

The auditorium was loud with families finding seats. Small boys in suits walked up and down the aisles handing out programs. Backstage, musicians gathered in small groups, holding their instruments, talking about each other's clothes.

"We won't wear black this year," Mom had announced to the orchestra earlier. "Let's have a very festive, happy, holiday orchestra for once."

And so, everyone was resplendent in bright colors. Even some of the boys, who were turned out in suits, wore colorful ties. Only Mom wore black, being the conductor.

Abi stood alone backstage, holding her instrument and reading through the program. Her eyes were glued to the bottom of the page. Right before the final piece of the evening, her solo was listed:

A Minor Concerto for Solo Violin .... *J. S. Bach*

Abigail Jane Crim

"Abi, you'll never believe it!" Tamika rushed up to her and grabbed her arm. "My Grandma Sunshine is here! She came!" Tamika's eyes were bright. "When I got home from school today, she was there. Dad had picked her up at the airport. I can't believe it."

Abi smiled widely. "That's great," she said, her heart full of everything that was wonderful that day. "Where is she?"

"She's with your grandma in the parking lot," Tamika said. "They made instant friends."

Abi laughed. "It's just like my grandma to do that." Abi wondered if Grandma Sunshine had told anyone about her letter. She hoped not.

"Look," Tamika said, "there they are."

Two old ladies, one black, one white, entered the auditorium. Abi's Grandma Johnson wore a Christmas green jumper with a red turtleneck. Sneakers on her feet.

"She always wears tennies," Abi said. "She says at her age, why worry about fashion?"

Tamika giggled. "Aren't they cute?"

Grandma Sunshine walked delicately, using her cane. She was a small woman, with rich dark skin and snow white hair. Her deep blue dress was covered with small embroidered flowers.

"She always embroiders," Tamika said. "She says hands with nothing to do will find trouble."

The girls approached, violins in hand, as the grandmas found seats in the front row.

"The better to see you, my dears," Grandma Johnson said.

"Grandma, this is my friend Abi," Tamika said.

Abi held out her hand. "It is so nice to meet you, Abi," Grandma Sunshine said. "And thank you very much. Without you I wouldn't have come."

Abi blushed.

"What do you mean, Grandma?" Tamika said, but Abi pulled her away.

"Come on," she said. "It's time to tune."

All the musicians were seated on the stage. Tamika tuned her violin at the piano, then mounted the stage and stood in front of the orchestra. She pulled a long, clear A. The instruments tuned. Abi helped a fourth grader behind her who did not know how to tune. Then she tuned her own instrument.

Abi's mother walked to the conductor's stand, smiled at the orchestra, then turned to the audience.

"Welcome to the Fairlawn Christian School Christmas Concert," she said. "We are so happy you have come. Please stand with me as Pastor Bennett leads us in prayer."

Pastor gave thanks to God for the Incarnation of the Lord Jesus Christ and for the preservation of the Word of God down through the centuries so that people today could read the Scriptures and understand the gospel of the grace of God. He prayed that the concert would honor the Lord and cause the listeners to meditate on Christ. He prayed that the musicians would have calmness of heart and the ability to play for God's glory.

The audience sat down amid a rustle of programs and shifting chairs. Mom turned to the orchestra, smiled, and gave the signal: Instruments up. The lights in the auditorium dimmed and the slow, soft music filled the room. Abi thought of the words as she played.

Away in a manger, no crib for His bed;
The little Lord Jesus laid down His sweet head.
The stars in the sky looked down where He lay;
The little Lord Jesus asleep on the hay.

Abi's hands and fingers played, but her mind could see the cold stable so long ago. The tiny baby, born to be King.

A hush followed the song. Mom smiled. Abi turned to the next song. And the next one, as hymn followed hymn. The winning duet played. Tamika played the section of "Thou Didst Leave Thy Throne" that Abi had done so poorly on, back at auditions in September. That seemed so long ago now. Abi wished Mrs. Cotton could be here now to hear them all play. She wondered what Mrs. Cotton was doing right now, how she was feeling, and whether the babies were still all right.

During intermission, Abi looked out at the audience from backstage. Refreshment tables were set up outside, and many of the adults had stepped outside to get cookies and coffee. Little girls in Christmas dresses spun around in the aisles.

There were Kimberly and her mother down front with Grandma Sunshine and Grandma Johnson. Kimberly was laughing at something Grandma Johnson had said. Will sat beside Dad, both of them sporting red bow ties that made Abi both cringe and smile. Thinking ahead to her solo, her hands shook slightly. She grabbed onto a stage curtain and looked around the audience again.

So many people were there. All her friends. Even Jerry and his parents were there, Jerry sitting next to his father, a tall man with a thoughtful face. Everyone was there except Mrs. Cotton. How much better if Mrs. Cotton had been able to come.

She would have been so proud of me.

Abi turned away from the audience. She caught a glimpse of herself in a backstage mirror, looked at herself from head to toe and smiled. "For once everything's perfect," she said to herself.

Tamika slid into the mirror image beside her. Resplendent in red velvet, she was stunning next to Abi's blue satin. They smiled at themselves in the mirror.

"You look nice," Tamika said.

"You too."

"Look at our grandmas," Tamika said, pulling Abi by the arm. They peered out at the audience again. The two old ladies were talking excitedly. Grandma Sunshine laughed.

"I'm glad I had that solo in the hymn," Tamika said. "In case Grandma doesn't come back. She was terribly frightened on the airplane. She said she prayed the whole way. And also, she is eighty-nine years old. Who knows if she'll ever hear me play again."

Abi thought back to her Grandpa Johnson. He'd never heard Abi play. She remembered the one time when she could have performed a simple piece for him. It was when she was seven years old and had just started taking violin lessons. Grandma and Grandpa had come to visit. *Play something for me, Sweet Pea,* Grandpa had said, but Abi had shaken her head no and run away, too nervous.

"And then he died," she said aloud.

"Who?" Tamika said.

"Oh, sorry," Abi said. "I was just thinking about my grandpa. He never heard me play."

The auditorium lights flashed, indicating that intermission would be over in three minutes. Tamika moved away to tune her instrument at the piano again. Some of the musicians took their places again on stage. But Abi lingered backstage, thinking about her grandpa and what Tamika had said. She wondered how she would feel if this was the only time Grandma Johnson would ever hear her play.

Now that she thought about it, it really was too bad Tamika hadn't won the honor solo. Tamika would have been wonderful, and her grandma had come so far to see her, overcoming her fear of traveling. No, she hadn't overcome her fear. She had been afraid and had come anyway.

"Jesu, Joy of Man's Desiring." It wasn't a hard piece, but the way Tamika played it on audition day had been truly beautiful. Abi knew she had won, and not Tamika, because her Bach concerto had been fiery and flashy, full of complicated timing, and fast. "Jesu, Joy of Man's Desiring" would be better for a Christmas concert though, she thought.

Most of the musicians were tuning by now, and she knew she should take her place in the front row of the second violins. But her heart had begun to pound hard, like it did when she stood on the high dive at the pool, trying to get up her nerve to jump off. Her hands sweated. She wiped them on the stage curtain so she wouldn't get sweat marks on her blue satin.

"You okay, honey?" Mom stood beside her, cool and beautiful in her long black conductor's dress. "Nervous about your solo?"

"Mom," she said, her voice unsteady, "this might be the only time Tamika's grandma ever gets to hear her play."

"Yes, Abi. That's true."

Abi turned and looked up at her mother with wide-open eyes. Could she do the impossible here? Could she give up what she'd earned, what was her right—her triumph—for her friend?

Behind them, on stage, Tamika played a long open A. Sounds of tuning filled the auditorium.

"Mom, could I . . ."

"Yes, Abi," Mom smiled and hugged her. "You could."

Abi's whole body trembled as she slid into her seat and tuned her violin. She watched Mom approach the concert-mistress's chair and speak quietly to Tamika. She saw

Tamika's eyes open wide, blinking hard. Then Tamika looked over at her and smiled. She mouthed, "Thanks, Abi."

Abi smiled. And, while she played through Christmas carols and the arrangement from Handel's *Messiah,* she wondered, Can a person be devastated with loss and yet be joyful for a friend at the same time? And answered herself: yes.

Mom turned to the audience.

"Before our final orchestra piece, 'Gloria in Excelsis Deo,' our honor soloist will play," she said. Mom paused and turned to the orchestra. She smiled at Abi and at Tamika.

"There is a change from what is listed in your program," she said. "In honor of her grandmother, Mrs. Sunshine Mitchell, Tamika Mitchell will play 'Jesu, Joy of Man's Desiring.' Tamika?"

Tamika rose and walked to the center of the stage. She began slowly, with deep resonance, her music—without accompaniment—filling the auditorium, tumbling over the audience like water, Abi thought, drenching them with beauty.

Abi looked from Tamika, beautiful in red velvet, to Grandma Sunshine in the front row. Grandma Sunshine's eyes were closed, tears running down her crinkly black cheeks. Then, the eyes opened, and Abi smiled widely as she watched Grandma Sunshine watch Tamika.

A week later, Abi got a letter in the mail. After she read it, she took it to her room. She pulled her treasure box from under her bed. She ran her finger over the writing on the lid that said *My Special Treasures* in gold crayon. She removed the top of the box and looked in. There were her first baby shoes. Her first report card. There were the beads from Tamika's party. And there was the tape of Grandpa's bassoon lullabies. Abi took out the letter she had just received. She read it over once more, then folded it up and slid it into the box. She replaced the box under her bed. Then she ran to Kimberly's to sit in the porch swing and predict everything wonderful.

Dear Abi, (the letter read)

I heard about your gift of the solo to Tamika, and I am profoundly grateful to know you, and to have been your teacher, if only for a little while. You set a new standard for friendship, and I know Tamika will always be thankful for what you did in giving her the honor solo. I know that I will always be deeply proud of you for this act of kindness.

Love,

Mrs. Cotton

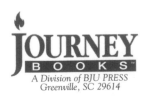